WAR BUDS 3

Overcome

JACK HUNT

DIRECT RESPONSE PUBLISHING

ISBN-13: 978-1548734459
ISBN-10: 1548734454

Dedication

For my family.

Prologue

Four months since fallout

Cyrus Ramsey slammed a magazine into his AR-15. After chambering a round, he brought the scope to his eye and scanned the desolate landscape on either side of Highway 395. He'd been waiting inside the two-man foxhole for the better part of an hour. A harsh wind nipped at his face, causing him to readjust his beanie to cover his ears. It was freezing, his breath clouded in front of his lips. It would soon be winter and survival was at the forefront of his mind. Supplies were at an all-time low even though they had managed to scavenge what little remained in surrounding towns, and steal the rest from unprepared travelers

Beside him, Damon Hartwig was fidgeting. The sound of a match striking a box made him turn his head. Damon cupped a hand near his mouth as he lit a cigarette.

"Put that out, they'll see the smoke."

Damon shook the match. "Who? Cyrus, we've been at this now for three days in a row and we haven't seen anyone."

"Put it out."

Damon pinched the end of it, then tucked the charred remainder behind his ear.

"Fuck's sake man, this is bullshit."

"You've got to have patience."

"Patience? I don't see why we don't just deploy the spike strips and keep one guy down here with the radio. They aren't going to be able to run anywhere. We could be here in less than twenty minutes."

Cyrus ignored him and got on the radio. Static crackled over the speaker.

"Victor, you got eyes on anyone?" he asked.

"Not yet."

They were positioned halfway between Mammoth and Bishop. It was roughly a forty-minute drive on an ordinary day. Victor and Joe were in a hole a quarter of a mile down the road. That main stretch of highway in the first two months had offered up numerous opportunities to prey upon the weak. Though with winter coming, fewer people were traveling by horse, foot or vehicle. Abandoned cars and trucks were dotted across the road like a scrapyard. Doors were open, baggage was scattered and gas had already been siphoned out. Desperate times had driven people to commit all manner of atrocities in order to survive. It wasn't personal. Since the fallout, the town of Mammoth Lakes had become nearly deserted. No one really knew how to cope with the blackout. Some fled, others stayed, many died.

Damon leaned his AR-15 up against the inside of the foxhole and climbed out.

"What are you doing?"

"Putting down the strip."

"Are you stupid?"

Damon wagged his finger in Cyrus's face. "I told you, don't call me that."

"Think, Damon. What use is a vehicle going to be to us if the tires are flat?"

He wasn't the brightest spark but they'd known each other since their short stint in the military. They'd both settled into life as mechanics in Mammoth Lakes and for the most part kept to themselves and tried to live out a meaningful existence until the shit storm of the century occurred. Since then they had banded together with friends and family to ensure they wouldn't go without.

Damon stormed over from the middle of the road with the strip in hand, and he tossed it back into the hole. "We should be out there, looking for them."

"And get yourself killed?" He shook his head. "It's about making smart choices. If they waltz into our neighborhood we'll handle them but I'm not going out of my way to start a war. Besides, do you honestly think they are faring any better than us?"

He shrugged and looked despondent. Cyrus sighed. "Go ahead and have the cigarette, just keep it low."

It didn't take much to put a smile on his face. It was the small things now, anything to provide a level of normality in a country that had collapsed. Without any communication with the outside, they hadn't been able to know what the level of danger was, who had attacked America or what they were facing beyond what they had learned so far. But right now it didn't matter. All that mattered was making sure they had that next meal, their weapons were loaded and they had enough supplies to make it through the fall and winter.

Victor's voice came back over the radio, it was low, almost a whisper.

"Cyrus. A target is approaching."

"How many?"

"Two. They're moving fast, Cyrus. Really fast."

He furrowed his brow. "Roger. Take out the second driver, we'll handle the first."

Two vehicles? The rumble of a truck could now be heard. Victor would usually take out the driver, causing the vehicle to go out of control, and Cyrus and Damon would finish off the remaining occupants, however, that was if there was one vehicle. More often than not, folks were traveling on horseback.

"How do you want to do this?" Damon asked. Cyrus scrambled out of the foxhole and stayed low in the tree line waiting for the sound of Victor's gunshot. In the past, they could usually take them out from the foxhole but this time there could be no room for error.

The truck was a blue Chevy 4 x 4; the one behind it was some old piece of crap that looked like it had seen better days. A trail of dust lifted behind them. They were gunning the engines as if they were being chased, except there was no one following.

The crack of Victor's rifle, and the sudden loss of control from the second truck was their signal to step out into the middle of the road. Both of them raised their AR-15's and unloaded a flurry of rounds at the windshield. In an instant, glass shattered and a red mist sprayed before the driver slumped and the vehicle swerved off to the right and crashed into the ditch. Metal crunched and flying dirt filled the air before it came to a grinding halt. The passenger side door flew open and a middle-aged man dropped out and returned fire before trying to flee.

It wasn't uncommon to see people fight back. It was the way the world was now. Who knew what their situation was? It was probably much like theirs — desperate. That's why Cyrus didn't think twice about killing a stranger. When it came down to it, it was their life or his. It wasn't like they hadn't encountered their fair share of roaming gangs who had shown up and tried to take from them. They hadn't once come across anyone willing to help them, so why would they?

"I've got him!" Damon said dropping to a knee, and squeezing the trigger twice. The first shot missed, the second struck him. His legs buckled and he landed hard, crying out in pain. As Damon moved in to finish him off,

Cyrus told him to wait.

"But…"

"I said wait!" Cyrus snapped. They hurried over to the man who had waded across a small river and made it a few feet up a steep embankment before he collapsed. Seeing them approach, his fingers raked at the soil in one final attempt to reach his rifle but it was out of reach. He flipped over just as Damon pressed a muddy boot against his bloody thigh.

Groaning in pain, and through gritted teeth he spoke, "Please. Take whatever you want. Just…"

Cyrus bent down cradling his rifle and looked at the man. He sniffed hard. "Why are you in such a hurry?"

"What?"

He genuinely seemed confused by the question.

"Speeding. Why were you speeding? Were you trying to get away from that other truck?"

"No," he said shaking his head. "That was my brother."

Tears welled up in his eyes. Were they genuine? No

one cared.

"So?" he probed him.

His face contorted. Confusion, agony and despair all rolled into one. "Don't you know?"

"What?"

He was getting a little impatient with the man acting so vague.

"Russian and North Korean troops have seized the city of Bishop. They are taking residents into custody and executing anyone who resists."

Cyrus sat back and stared at him blankly. Was he having a mental breakdown? Troops occupying? He knew the country was at war and they had suffered a nuclear attack, but troops on U.S. soil? Russians and Koreans? And why the hell would they be in Mono County? There was nothing here for them.

"And you managed to escape?" Damon asked.

"We weren't in the city. We have a farm on the outskirts. My brother saw the soldiers arrive. Paratroopers. Some arrived in trucks."

Cyrus didn't know what to make of it. Was the guy delirious? Was he trying to sell them a line in the hope that they would have mercy on him? He was going to die either way, as they didn't leave anyone behind. And they sure as hell didn't give anyone a free pass. That was a rookie mistake.

"How many?"

Damon stifled a laugh and Cyrus glared at him. He knew he thought it was a joke but after the shit the country had just gone through, it wasn't a far stretch of the imagination to think that whoever had dropped the nukes would eventually follow through with a full-scale invasion.

"How the fuck should I know? We didn't stick around to count them." He groaned as Damon applied pressure to his wound. "Please. No. There was a lot. That's all I know."

"That's all you know?"

He nodded. Without missing a beat Cyrus straightened up and fired a round through the man's skull. They turned and walked away without a second thought. Killing had become the norm. Keeping people alive only meant more mouths to feed and they were already scraping the bottom of the barrel trying to stay alive themselves.

"You think he's full of shit?" Damon asked as they crossed the river and made their way over to where Victor and Joe were going through the second truck and pulling out anything that was of use.

"Well, there is only one way to find out."

Damon looked at him and frowned. "We aren't going anywhere near it."

"No? And what if he was telling the truth? If they've moved this far north, it won't be long before they reach Mammoth and then what? Our only advantage is to find out."

"Hey Cyrus," Victor held up a six-pack of Budweisers. That was all Damon needed to distract him.

"Are you kidding me?" Damon hollered, hurrying over. Victor tossed him one and he cracked it open and chugged it down in one go. Cyrus didn't take one. His focus shifted to the road that wound its way off into the distance, towards Bishop. They were a good twenty minutes away. Had the men been spotted heading this way? If they had, it wouldn't be long before soldiers would be heading their way, if there were any.

Their group of eleven had survived so far because they hadn't encountered anyone capable of giving them real trouble, well, except for a small group they had a run-in with a few months back but they had all but vanished.

"Cyrus. Cyrus." Victor repeated his name to get his attention while holding out a beer. He took it and cracked it open but didn't drink it. His mind was occupied by the dead man's words.

"What is it?" Victor asked.

"He thinks troops are on the ground," Damon said letting out a chuckle. Cyrus ignored him. Whether it was true or not, he didn't like surprises and he certainly wasn't going to ignore the stranger. They were speeding for a reason, and there was only one reason anyone shifted ass now and that was a threat against their life.

"Victor, take the second vehicle and drive it into the tree line, stash it out of sight. We're going to pay Bishop a visit and see for ourselves."

"Are you serious?"

As if snapping out of a trance, Cyrus turned and glanced at him. He didn't need to raise his voice or lose control to make it clear that he wasn't screwing around. They had all known him long enough.

"Okay." He jogged over to the truck and drove it out of view.

"You know, the other truck has several cases of baby food. Not exactly my idea of good food but you can't be picky now," Joe said. Cyrus cut him off as he was about to continue.

"Joe, drag the driver out of the other truck and bring it around."

He didn't argue and just went to it. Damon however wasn't as easy to convince. Their entire lives he'd questioned Cyrus over his decisions. If he wanted to go left, Damon usually had three reasons why they should go right. It didn't matter if going right was a dumb move or not. He got off on doing the opposite, usually to get a rise out of Cyrus.

"Look, Cyrus, I'm all for seeing if he's telling the truth but shouldn't we wait until this evening?"

"We might not have until then."

"And if they see us?"

Cyrus backhanded his stomach. "Grow a pair."

He heard Damon exhale hard as Cyrus turned back towards the road and finished off the beer. He didn't want to believe that troops were beginning to occupy America but they had to be prepared for the worst. Joe pulled around the truck, and they waited for Victor to join them before heading towards Bishop.

* * *

Cyrus had Victor pull off a few miles from the city. He knew the area well as he'd spent the first ten years of his life in Bishop before his father took a job in Mammoth. They cut through a farmer's field, and he had him bring the truck around to the back of a home. They parked there and crossed through a field to a large area called Millpond Recreation Area. Moving at a crouch they threaded their way around trees until they crested a rise. Cyrus brought up a pair of binoculars and scanned the western side of Bishop. He nodded slowly.

"Let me take a look." Damon was eager to see for himself.

Sure enough the place was occupied by troops. It was hard to tell how many there were as they were spread out and from the looks of it had set up two checkpoints on U.S. Highway 395 and Red Hill Road. Damon lowered the binoculars and looked over to Cyrus who had pulled out a cigarette. He stared at it like it was his last and rolled it between his fingers before placing it into his lips and lighting it.

"What does this mean?"

"What the fuck do you think it means?" Victor said taking a turn to look through the binoculars. "We are at war."

"No. I mean. What do we do now?"

Cyrus had no idea. His mind was reeling and still processing it all. This changed everything. It was no longer about preparing to survive the winter. They were going to need help, but they had all but burned their bridges with those in Mammoth.

"That group we encountered. Where did you last see them?" Cyrus asked Damon.

"On the west side of town — Crestwood Hills."

Chapter 1

Forty-eight hours later

Walker was a shithole in the middle of nowhere. An hour and twenty minutes north of Mammoth Lakes, the small town had boasted a population of seven hundred and twenty-one before the fallout. Now it was deserted. At least that's what they thought when they entered early that morning searching for supplies. They'd got into the habit of going out twice a week to surrounding towns to see what they could scavenge. Food and water was a top priority yet they would take anything that was useful. Even though Mack had well stocked the camp at Iron Mountain there were now twenty mouths to feed. When they weren't hunting animals or searching nearby towns, they worked in rotating shifts patrolling the area.

Brody felt the noose tighten around his neck. Chase

was beside him.

"Ever had one of those déjà vu moments?" Chase said grimacing as the two large men pushed them forward towards the edge of what appeared to be a new building. They shuffled forward, their wrists and ankles bound tight.

"I gotta say, this is a very unorthodox method of hanging," Brody remarked.

"Shut the hell up," the heavily bearded man said.

"I knew we shouldn't have come here," Chase added.

Twenty minutes earlier they had split up. Kai, Marlin and Todd were somewhere else. No doubt swigging back expensive bourbon as Marlin had his eyes on the local bar from the moment they set foot in the town. It wasn't your typical town that had a stretch of shops. It was all spread out along Highway 395 and throughout the foothills.

Brody tried to bargain with the men. "Listen guys, can't we just talk? We can offer you weapons, warm food and shelter. It can't be good trying to survive out here."

A sharp jab to the back of his ribs was the answer to that. Brody groaned and pressed forward. The two men had been pretty smart. They had observed them arrive, and waited until they split up before they attacked. Brody had managed to stab one of them in the leg before the other knocked him out. By the time Chase showed up to find out what the commotion was, it was too late. They had the entire town rigged up with traps by the looks of it. That's how they'd managed to pull the wool over his eyes when he entered the dusty old store. He'd only taken a few steps inside when the floorboards collapsed, and he found himself in the basement getting a pummeling.

One of them spat a wad of phlegm. "We have what we need here."

"But surely you have to share it with the others?"

They laughed between themselves. "Others?"

"That answers that question."

Brody stopped a few feet away from the edge of the two-story building.

"You know… Eventually you are going to run out of supplies, what then? Listen, I get it. We are in a shit storm. No one understands protecting what you have more than us but we need to work together. How about a name?"

"How about you shut the fuck up?" the grizzled-looking man said shoving him forward. They were both wearing camo clothing that looked as if it had been stolen from an army surplus store. They had Glocks in holsters on their legs, and were wielding serrated knives. Their faces were painted up like they had just stepped out of the Vietnam War. These weren't just ordinary people. They were prepared, resourceful, the kind of folks that would have made a great addition to the camp at Iron Mountain.

Since leaving Crestwood Hills, they had been trying to come up with different ways to rig up traps, not only to catch animals, but also to prevent any unpleasant surprises in the night. Iron Mountain was located northwest of Mammoth. The reason they hadn't been able to find it on the map was because Iron Mountain was the name Mack had given to the place when he purchased land there. It was actually located between Deer Mountain, White Wing Mountain and San Joaquin Mountain. It was a beautiful spot protected by wilderness and nestled in the Inyo National Forest.

"I need a piss," Chase muttered.

"Won't matter in a minute," the man said forcing them up onto the lip of the building. "Though feel free to go now." Even though it was only two stories it seemed a long way down. Their necks would break, that was for sure.

Brody's eyes scanned the town for any sign of the others. Where were they?

As they pushed Chase forward he jerked backwards.

"Shit! The rope is not long enough."

"What? Didn't you bring extra?" the other man replied.

"We haven't used this in a while."

"Well go get some more."

He huffed as he ambled away.

"At least you can go over." The other one gripped Brody hard and went to shove him but he resisted.

"Don't I get any last words or a request?"

"What do you think this is?"

"Come on, man."

The guy had a firm grip on the back of Brody's jacket, all it would take was a slight shove and he would be gone.

"Allow me to go with my friend."

He was delaying the inevitable but if it ended here, he'd prefer to die at the same time as Chase. Dying alone didn't thrill him. Heck, dying at all wasn't on his list when he woke up that morning. For a short while he had gone back and forth on whether to visit Walker. It probably didn't help that he and Rodriguez had been tangled up beneath the sheets. Things were just beginning to get good. He'd got to know Isabel better and Ava had taken a liking to her. Now here he was inches away from death's door.

The bearded guy sneered and pulled him back from the edge. "I guess a few more minutes isn't going to matter."

Chase arched his eyebrows. Now where are you, guys? Brody thought.

* * *

Ten minutes earlier Todd was standing in front of a sign that gave the hours for Walker Country Store. His mouth was watering as he stared at the foot-long sub sandwich shown below the deli hours. It was packed with ham, tomatoes, cheese and lettuce. He hadn't seen anything that looked that good in months. His stomach was grumbling and he was becoming sick and tired of eating cans of beans and deer meat.

"Subs. Pizza. Beer. It seems almost unreal now."

"Stop torturing yourself and give us a hand looking around this place."

"I don't know why we're even bothering, this town doesn't look as if it had much to begin with. I mean can it even be called a town? We've only seen four stores and most of those were stripped bare. I really think we should take a trip up to Carson City. There is bound to be way more to choose from up there."

"Yeah and while we're at it, let's book into a spa and get our nails trimmed," Marlin said in jest as he cradled his rifle and slid in through the shattered window trying not to cut himself up.

"Make it quick, we should really get back to the other guys. I don't like splitting up," Kai said.

"Ah, what, you need someone to hold your hand?" Marlin scoffed and flicked on his flashlight. Even though it was light outside, inside the store it was dark and dingy. It smelled musty, and had the faint smell of urine lingering in the air.

"This place is nasty."

"What do you expect after four months? Air conditioning and a sexy waitress asking to take your order?" Todd remarked. Someone had torn down the shelves and broken apart the metal.

"What about gas?"

"The pumps aren't going to work."

"I know that, dipshit, I'm saying there might be some left in the gas tanks underground. Those usually will hold several thousand gallons. I doubt someone managed to siphon all of it out."

"Well, knock yourself out. There is a hose in the back of the truck, get sucking!" Marlin let out a laugh and wandered off into the back of the store. Kai looked at Todd.

"Don't look at me. I can still taste the last lot that we brought up. I'm not doing that again." No one really wanted to do it. Most of the time they ended up swallowing some of it if they weren't careful. It was easier to siphon from vehicles, or visit emergency service locations such as hospitals, fire stations or police departments as many of those kept stores of fuel on hand.

Kai shook his head and walked away while Todd hopped over the counter and began rooting around underneath where the cash register would have been. There was nothing. Someone had stripped it bare. Not even a crumb had been left behind or a packet of cigarettes. He hadn't had one in several days and was starting to get a little desperate for a nicotine fix.

"You found anything?" Todd called out to Marlin.

"Nothing."

He could hear him breaking apart boxes in the back of the store, and Kai cursing outside. As Todd waded through the clutter and debris that littered the floor he picked up a sign that once would have sold for twenty bucks. It read: *Don't Cry Because It's Over, Smile Because It Happened.* He snorted and tossed it across the room. Like he was going to smile because the country had collapsed. Everywhere he turned he found more signs with dumb phrases all over them. At one time he might have considered buying one for his mother. She was into that kind of crap.

"I would kill for some moldy bread. I don't care if it it's gone completely green. Anything to change up what we've been having."

Marlin didn't reply. At first he didn't give it a

thought. Todd figured he had his nose in some box full of pornos. His foot struck another sign on the floor, this one read: *Every Moment Matters*. Like hell it does, he thought as he kicked it across the floor. Three months of living on the bare essentials had caused all of them to lose weight. It didn't help that he had a pain in his tooth. At some point he was going to need to get that looked at, or extract that damn thing.

"Marlin."

Again nothing. He jerked his head to the side and listened intently. He could hear movement. He was out there but why wasn't he responding? Todd reached for his Glock and kept it low as he approached the back room. Using the tip of his foot he eased the door open while bringing his weapon up to chest height but keeping it close to his body. As the door swung open, he exhaled hard. Sitting in the middle of the room was Marlin, tucking into several packets of chips.

"Are you kidding me?"

"What?" he said with his mouth loaded. Some of

the chips were spilling over his lips.

"So you were just going to have them all to yourself?"

"No, I was going to save a few."

"What? The scraps at the bottom of the bag?" Todd lunged forward and grabbed the bag of Doritos out of his hands. He shoved a few into his mouth. They weren't crisp, which meant they had probably been a half-eaten, discarded pack or the leftovers from a batch that had expired.

"Save some for Kai," he said.

"Says the guy who was about to eat the whole damn lot," Todd mumbled while filling his face. He couldn't get them in his mouth fast enough. Marlin had started on the next bag and leaned back against the wall. "You think—"

Before he could spit the words out, Kai came rushing in yelling for them to come quick.

"What's going on?"

"I heard gunshots coming from farther down."

"It's probably just some loon letting off some steam. Here, you want a pack?" Marlin held out a pack, oblivious to the fact that Brody and Chase might have been coming under attack. Todd dropped his pack and headed out with Kai, while Marlin protested.

"Can't I get a moment of peace around here?"

Outside it was silent.

"Which way?"

Kai pointed and they hopped into the truck and swerved out.

"Did you get gas?"

"Half a canister before I heard the shots."

By the time they reached the area where they had last seen Chase and Brody, not a sound could be heard. Kai parked around the back of the new hardware store and they moved out at a crouch. From where they were situated they could hear voices but not see anyone. Kai inched his way up to a window and looked inside. It was dark inside but he could make out the silhouette of two people and then he heard Chase's voice. A struggle and then… he ducked. One of the men looked towards the back and they could hear his boots getting close. Kai readied his gun, expecting him to come out of the back door but it didn't open.

They waited there for what felt like five minutes but it was probably closer to a minute while they discussed what they were going to do. Marlin said he was going around to the side and would go up the fire escape, while Todd and Kai would enter through the back.

Todd went first, pulling back the door so Kai could enter. He slid around to the right while Todd took the left side. With the windows covered by shutters, it provided enough darkness to cover them as they shuffled towards a staircase that led up to a second floor.

"Shit! The rope is not long enough."

"Didn't you bring extra?"

"We haven't used this in a while."

"Well go get some more."

That's what they heard before the sound of boots crunching against metal, then glass. Kai made a gesture with his head as he slid around the side of the staircase and waited for the stranger to appear. The problem was he didn't emerge. He stopped halfway down the stairs. There was no way he could see them, they were shrouded by darkness, and out of sight. Not a sound could be heard.

Then, Todd looked up, that's when he saw the guy. He'd stopped because he could see them in the oval security mirror in the corner of the room. Todd brought his gun around as the guy squeezed off two shots in his direction.

* * *

"What the hell?" The bearded guy rushed towards the emergency staircase. He glanced back only for a second to keep an eye on Brody and Chase. At the doorway, he pulled it open.

"Doug?"

"There are two of them," his friend shouted back.

More shots echoed from below, and Brody smiled knowing it was them. The guy swiveled around looking super pissed off and began crossing the rooftop heading for them. By the look on his face, it was clear that he fully intended to throw them off regardless of whether or not he had enough rope.

He'd made it about halfway across the roof when he froze as gunshots snapped near his feet. Brody turned to see Marlin on the far side of the roof. The guy didn't stand a chance but instead of firing back at Marlin, he took cover behind a metal air vent and placed his weapon down.

"I'm unarmed. Don't shoot."

"Is this guy for real?" Chase said.

It was hard to believe that only a few seconds ago he was prepared to hang them and now he was getting fired upon he was giving up. They'd never seen anything like it. Every single time they encountered someone who was a threat, they fought back. He extended his hands but didn't come around the vent. There was something about his willingness to give up his firearm that didn't seem right. Chase and Brody shuffled across the roof, away from the edge and in the direction of Marlin as he beckoned them on.

The door on the stairwell burst open as the second guy emerged. He didn't look back to see that his buddy had decided to wave the white flag. Instead he was trying to tie off the door with a chain.

"Travis, a little help."

Right then he turned and saw that Travis had his hands out. His eyes bounced over to Brody and then he caught sight of Marlin pointing a rifle at his head.

"One breath and it's over," Marlin said. That momentary distraction was all Travis needed. He didn't go for the gun he'd tossed down as he had another on him. He wheeled around the other side in one smooth motion, just as Brody shouted for them to drop.

The gun erupted and his buddy managed to rush over to where they were. Now both of them were behind the large vent. Brody and Chase were on their bellies trying to roll over to where Marlin was. As they were doing that, the door to the stairwell burst open and Kai was the first one out. A sudden snap of bullets and they retreated. Once Chase had managed to get over to where Marlin was, he cut their binds and handed Brody a Glock.

"Travis," Brody called out. "This doesn't have to end in blood."

"Of course it does."

"You're good at trapping, right?"

"Stop trying to reach me."

"You could have launched me off that roof but you didn't. Why?"

There was silence as if he was contemplating an answer.

"Come on now. You didn't have to wait for him to return."

"Common courtesy," was his response.

Brody nodded slowly. "Listen up, we could use two guys like you."

"What?" Chase spluttered, his eyes widening. "Are you out of your mind?" he said in a whisper. "They just tried to kill us."

Marlin also looked disturbed by what Brody was saying.

"They weren't going to kill us."

"Oh no, so that noose around our neck was just for kicks."

"Chase, if they wanted us dead, they could have just shot us."

"Malcolm could have done the same but he chose to hang and slice people up. Some people get off on seeing people suffer."

"Sure, but think about it. They were able to unarm both of us without firing a single shot. Those are the kind of men we could use. People with skills."

"I'm sorry, Brody, but that's bullshit. We are not taking them back with us."

"He's right, Brody," Marlin said. "It's too much risk."

"There are only twenty of us. We need to start thinking about recruiting people."

Chase looked around the corner. The men kept peeking out but didn't look as if they were ready to attack.

"More mouths to feed? You have finally lost it."

"No, because we need to start looking beyond ourselves. We trusted Gus and look how that worked out. He's one of our best sharpshooters."

"That's different."

"How? He tried to kill me and Daniel."

"I wouldn't have brought him back," Marlin said.

"Well we did, and it's worked out real well."

Chase frowned. "Not everyone is like Gus."

"But how can we know unless we take that risk?" Brody asked. "Look, I'm not having this conversation with you right now. I think these two could come in handy."

"What? As executioners? Fuck that. I'm dropping these assholes."

Marlin went to get up and Brody grabbed a hold of his arm. "Wait!"

"For what?"

Still holding his arm he peered around the stairwell and called out to the two men.

"Travis!"

As he tried to get their attention, he didn't realize that Kai and Todd had circled back around and come up the side of the building using the fire escape. This placed them directly behind the men. One moment there was silence, then the next, an explosion of gunfire. Just like that it was over. Marlin punched the air. "Now that's how you do it. Well done, guys."

Brody just stared at the bodies, and then his eyes met Chase's.

"You know it had to be done."

On one hand they were right. They couldn't trust strangers. And yet at some point they would need to if they were to survive what was coming.

Chapter 2

Marine Sergeant Ronan Westbury gazed into the flames. The truck had been filled with Russian soldiers. They'd ambushed them on the outskirts of Gardnerville just south of Carson City. His platoon had been reduced from thirty-five down to seventeen after a ferocious firefight. Their orders had been to prevent them seizing towns and to ensure the safety of civilians. They were one of many platoons that were deployed along the east and west sides of America. The nuclear attack had decimated some key areas and caused an untold loss of life but it hadn't crippled the U.S. military or the entire power grid. Certain areas stretching from Michigan to Idaho and Louisiana to Utah were still in operation. Word had reached them before communication went down that U.S. central command was holding back the tide of attacks on the East Coast, though with no communication now on the west, it was all hearsay.

"Brooks, any confirmation on where that second unit was headed?"

"Southeast, Sarge. Griffin and Vaughn are the only men that have survived. The rest of the platoon was wiped out. Looks like they have taken the city of Bishop and set up a perimeter."

"Get the guys ready, we are rolling out to help them."

"But what about Gardnerville?"

He cast a glance over his shoulder at the town of five thousand strong that had been turned to rubble by intense warfare.

"There's nothing more we can do here. I'm not leaving them down there."

After ten years serving in the Marines he had been on numerous tours, been through a breakdown of a marriage and seen many of his brothers in arms buried. And still nothing came close to this. He knew this day was coming. Like most in the military their job wasn't to question the powers that be but to remain ready for deployment at a moment's notice.

He looked at the tired faces of his men who'd been up for close to twenty-six hours. Nothing burned him more than to leave behind those who had fallen but they were racing against the clock. Every hour foreign troops were pushing inland. Months prior to the threats posed by North Korea, they had been deployed on an armada of ships sent towards North Korea. It was meant to be a "show of force." He scoffed as he got into one of two tan military trucks along with the others. The U.S. hadn't banked on the Russians taking advantage of North Korea's initial attack. They were the first wave, followed by the Russians. It was to be expected. The relationship that the U.S. had with Russia had never settled. It was shaky at best. But they didn't expect China to get involved. Though they had yet to see Chinese troops, they would be ready if and when they showed their faces. It infuriated them to think that the U.S. had been so gullible as to believe that they were an ally. After a report had come out that China had hacked into the THAAD anti-missile system, that should have been their warning. But no, it was swept under the rug. Had they acted then, they might have been able to prevent the ballistic missiles from destroying thousands of U.S. troops. Had they intervened when China took retaliatory measures against South Korean companies after the joint decision made by the U.S. and South Korea, perhaps the first wave of nukes wouldn't have reached the U.S.

"Commie bastards!" Rocco muttered to himself, taking out a cigarette and lighting it. "I can't wait to fucking kill them all."

"You are aware that the Communist Party has not been in power for over two decades in Russia," Parker said.

"Who cares? We should have nuked them back in the '80s, along with China and that asshole in North Korea. But no, we have to take the diplomatic approach. Look where it's got us. Now if we had handled it the way we did with the Japs after World War Two, we wouldn't be in this position."

"How so?"

Westbury listened to his men shoot the breeze as the heavily armored truck rumbled its way south.

"Well they were forbidden from having any kind of standing army, just some forces for their own self-defense. The U.S. has basically protected their asses ever since."

"They do have an army. It's not big but it's in the top ten and is one of the most advanced armies in the world," Martinez added.

"Whatever. You don't see them getting involved and you would think if anyone had a grudge against the U.S. it would be them. Nope. What do we do? We spend all our time funneling our money into having our boys protect the damn Afghani poppy fields." He rubbed his thumb and finger together. "And you know why. Money. Opium."

"Dude, you have it backwards. We were eradicating the fields but then the Taliban started seizing it all so we had to step in because it was the livelihood of the farmers in Marja."

"Anyway, what the hell has that got to do with this invasion?"

"Everything."

He didn't elaborate any further and just looked out one of the windows. Tension was high and they were looking for someone to blame. Heading south on Highway 395, Westbury fished around in one of his pockets and retrieved the photo of his eleven-year-old boy, Dustin. Despite the divorce he'd remained on good terms with his ex and had shared custody. His home was in Reno, and he'd been in the middle of a three-week vacation when he got the call. At first he thought it was just another deployment overseas, then he learned about the nuke threats.

"Sarge," Martinez pointed to a blockade of vehicles that were clogging up the road. It looked as if someone had purposely put them in place. Martinez eased off the gas.

"Well go around it."

There was nothing but hilly landscape covered in

sagebrush for miles on either side of the road. A blue sky stretched out before them, with a few fluffy clouds dotted throughout. Though it was sunny, it was deceiving as it was cold as hell outside.

Martinez took the truck off to the side, and navigated around the right side of the convoys of vehicles that had been shifted into place to create a wall across the road. Barbed wire, and all manner of steel poles and shit had been wrapped around and through the frames to create an impenetrable barrier. On the left side, no one would have been able to drive around it as there was a steep incline but to the right, it was a little easier.

"They've well placed this, hold on, it's going to get bumpy."

The sound of metal grinding against metal as the truck struck the corner of one and forced it out of the way was matched by the sound of gunfire. All of them reacted fast as the truck came under heavy fire.

"Are these fools for real?"

The bullets were pinging off the sides. There was

no way they could penetrate the armored vehicle that was a cross between an MRAP, a Humvee and an M-ATV armed with a .50 Cal.

"What do you want to do, Sarge?"

"Don't slow down, just keep going." He turned to Rocco. "Get up there and salute them back, I'm sure they're just thanking us for our service."

Rocco slid up behind the M-240 machine gun and began unloading a shitload of lead their way. He started laughing his head off. "Oh you have got to see these assholes."

The rest of the guys leaned across and looked out of the thin slots. Outside there were four guys carrying AR-15s and dressed in combat gear. One of them had a red bandanna around his head as if he thought he was Rambo. *What a prick!* As rounds tore up the ground near their feet, they scrambled falling over each other to get out of the line of fire. It was fucking hilarious.

"Another bunch of wannabe soldiers. How many more of these assholes are we going to come across?"

"Before this war is over, tons."

It wasn't the first time they had come across roving gangs, or small clusters of folks who were trying to stake their claim on turf and vehicles in operation. What they were driving was like gold. He just wished for once they came across someone with a lick of sense. Firing Remington ammo at an armored vehicle — now that was just stupid.

Rocco ceased fire and dropped back down. "Oh that was just fun."

"Well don't get too comfortable. There is a good chance most of us aren't going to be around in a few days. I hope you guys have made peace with your maker."

Martinez pulled out a silver cross around his neck, kissed it and muttered a few words in Spanish before gunning the engine. Westbury wasn't a religious man growing up, but since joining the military, he had realized that it wasn't a bad thing to have some belief in a higher power. He just hadn't managed to get on board with the whole reading a Bible or praying. His prayers usually involved a lot of f-bombs and occurred only when hot lead was being fired in his direction.

"Sarge, you think we stand a chance?"

Whitlock was only twenty-one years of age. Still wet behind the ears, and with only one tour overseas, he looked like he should have been working in IT, tucked safely behind a desk. Instead, he was here busting his ass.

"Of dying, yeah."

"That's not what I meant."

"I know," he replied before returning to gazing out at the desolate landscape.

Chapter 3

Mack had spared no expense when creating the bug-out location on Iron Mountain. He'd purchased a piece of land in a very specific place, an area that seemed strange even to the owner who sold it. According to Bridget, he'd tried to sell Mack a piece of land closer to Mammoth Lakes, trails and Highway 395. Of course, he was thinking convenience, Mack was thinking survival.

Brody veered off 395 onto Deadman Creek Road. It was dusty and so off the beaten path that it seemed more like a walking trail than a road. They drove west as far as the road would take them until it came to an end just southwest of White Wing Mountain. There they stored the truck in the heavily forested area of the Inyo National Forest using camouflage mesh netting and tree limbs. It wasn't perfect but the location was. The only types of people who would have made their way down that road were hikers and campers and since this event, they hadn't seen a single one.

From there it was a good forty-minute hike to the camp.

Along the way Brody thought back to what Mack had taught them about having a secondary location to retreat to in the event they needed to escape. He had taught them about the seven essentials: location distance, water availability, concealment, escape, self-reliance, land property cost and potential threats from the weather.

Essentially, location mattered for the obvious reasons of security and self-sufficiency. There was no point buying a cottage in the middle of a heavily populated area as it wouldn't take long for people to come knocking and when push came to shove there likely wouldn't be any way to sustain oneself long-term due to a lack of natural resources. That's why Mack chose a location that was easily accessible and yet far enough away from high-density population areas that it would be safe. Safety was critical, and so was being able to escape, that's why he'd selected a location that had three routes of entry and escape. You see, the way Mack saw it, if law enforcement or the National Guard closed the major arteries, the location still could be reached from any one of the three roads that led into Deadman Creek Road. Now of course that was taking into consideration transportation. If they weren't using a vehicle they could reach the location from any direction, simply by hiking.

Concealment, self-reliance and water availability were also vital for survival.

The camp itself was designed to hold up to twenty people, yet it had room for expansion. Four cabins were partially built into a rocky bluff, which helped keep the residents cool in the summer and shielded from the elements in the winter. As it was surrounded by dense forest, it also meant that the chances of prying eyes seeing the camp from above or at a distance were slim.

Next, was its proximity to two lakes. Having a cistern or some kind of water storage was handy but nearby rivers and lakes were vital for long-term sustainability. Streams were good but they had the potential of drying up and a mild drought could mean certain death. The fact was they had no idea how long they were going to be there, and Mack knew that. He was prepared long before the shit hit the fan.

The land itself was perfect for building, farming and hunting and if needed they could sustain themselves there indefinitely without ever venturing out to surrounding towns. But getting out was important for their own sanity, and especially if they were to keep their finger on the pulse of the evolving situation.

As they trudged back through the forest, each of them was occupied with his own thoughts. It was strange to see how four months could change them. In the hours after the nuke strikes, confusion had dominated their minds. Two weeks later, reliance on one another was noticeable and now four months out they were each voicing opinions over what was best for the group as a whole. No one person determined the direction they would head in, or what the others would abide by. So far that had worked, yet Brody was now beginning to think that it might become their undoing.

"I don't understand why you would have let them live," Kai said. He'd been chewing at the bit to go over it with Brody after hearing about it from Marlin. "They tried to kill you. Hell, if we hadn't shown up, you would both be hanging from your necks back there."

"Maybe, maybe not."

Chase kicked at the soil as they trudged around tall trees. The leaves had already morphed from rich green to golden browns and many had fallen. In a few months they would be tackling snow and so they were hoping to stock up on as much food as they could. Over the summer months they had tilled the earth, planted vegetables and created a storehouse of dried meat. There was plenty to eat but they were mindful that they would have to make it stretch until the spring.

"You know better than anyone else. No one can be trusted now," Chase muttered.

"And what happens if we encounter another situation like the one with Malcolm? What then?"

"We'll handle it just the way we did the first time around."

"We had help, Chase. If it wasn't for those we met along the way, who knows how successful we would have been? Not everyone out there is the enemy."

"But do you want to take that chance?"

"Yes. Yes I do. We are not an island. Society wasn't meant to live this way. If we are to eventually rebuild, we are going to have to trust others."

Marlin cradled his rifle like a baby and glanced up at the sky. "Trust is earned."

"I agree but how do you expect anyone to earn it when we don't give them a chance?"

"Brody, for God's sake, they had their chance," he said spinning around. "We gave them the opportunity to leave with us but no, instead they dragged us up onto that roof and were about to toss us off. Just because you managed to talk Gus into helping, that doesn't mean you can do the same with everyone we encounter."

"Everyone? There were two of them."

"And what about that young guy back in June Lake? If it wasn't for Marlin, you would have been dead."

Brody glanced at Marlin but he said nothing. They had entered June Lake a few weeks back and stumbled across a kid, no older than twenty-two. At first he seemed like he was in dire straits. No shoes on, wandering the street asking for handouts. Brody took pity on him and offered to take him back. What he didn't realize was the guy was carrying an eight-inch serrated blade. If it hadn't been for Marlin's quick reaction, he would have plowed it deep into the back of his neck.

He sighed. There was truth to what they were saying. He wasn't stupid; he knew that the attack had changed people. Those who would have never turned on others would now kill in a New York minute. But that didn't mean they had to turn their back on everyone in need.

"I get what you were trying to do, man, but we've got to take care of ourselves."

"Screw the rest," Brody said, saying what he wanted

to hear.

"Exactly."

Brody scoffed. He was going to debate it further but as they got closer to the camp, Ava came rushing out. He scooped her up and then put her back down again.

A smile came over his hardened features. "You are getting way too big to carry."

"Did you find any?" she asked with eager anticipation.

She'd wanted him to bring back some candy bars, and he had every intention of doing so until they got distracted and encountered the two maniacs. He tossed a hand up. "Sorry, hon, things didn't go exactly to plan."

"Hey kiddo," Marlin said. She turned her head and he tossed a candy bar towards her. Her face lit up as she caught it. "And there are plenty more where they come from."

Marlin eyed Brody as Ava gave him a hug before running back towards the camp.

"Thanks," Brody said as they entered the camp.

The entrance required climbing over a series of rocky boulders and squeezing through what they had named "the letterbox." It was a thin vertical gap in an outcropping of rocks. From the top of each boulder, they could see for miles. Once through, Kai and Todd moved back into place a series of bushes and rocks that both secured and concealed the entrance.

"Back in Narnia, now where is Mr. Tumnus?" Marlin said before dropping his backpack and stretching.

Marlin was in the habit of calling the place Narnia because of how it opened up on the other side and was almost like a world in itself. He'd given Officer Dolman the nickname of Mr. Tumnus as he said he resembled him now that he'd grown a rough-looking goatee and had wild curly hair.

They'd recently constructed a new building all made from logs. It wasn't much to look at, and it only seated ten of them but it was Dolman's pet project. Something to keep him sane, he said. He wanted a command center, somewhere they could set up the ham radio, and deal with issues as they arose. Todd wanted it kitted out with some kind of music system that ran off the solar-powered generator but Dolman wouldn't allow it.

"There he is, the man himself." Marlin fished into his bag and pulled out a bottle of brandy. "I thought you might enjoy this. You still have those Cuban cigars?"

"Oh you devil. Where did you dig that up?"

He was busy finishing off a section of the building. He laid down a hammer and wiped his brow with a white cloth and ambled over. Marlin handed him the bottle and glanced back at Brody. "Found it in a storehouse belonging to two head cases who Brody wanted to invite back. Ain't that right, brother?"

Brody shook his head and wandered off into one of the cabins. Unlike a typical cabin, this had a very open concept. Mack was a minimalist. Instead of investing his money in creating separate rooms in every cabin, he simply hooked up hammock-style beds and filled the rest of the open space with wicker armchairs. Something that was light, easy to move around and durable. It meant he could invest his money where it was needed most, in a battery bank and a powerful back-up generator that was powered both by diesel and solar.

Since moving in, a few of them had hooked up thick Persian-style rugs that were rolled up around a pole on the ceiling. With a tug of a cord, they would drop down and provide some privacy. The only ones that had anything better than that were those who were couples. They slept and lived in the largest cabin that could house up to twelve people, more if they squeezed an extra person into each of the rooms. According to Bridget, that was the only cabin out there for years until he expanded it and created the additional ones. She'd probed him over why he needed them and he said, you never know who's going to show up for supper. Just as well, as it would have been a tough fit getting all twenty of them into the one cabin. They already felt as if they were living on top of each other, it was one of the reasons why Brody was keen to venture out each week. It gave him time to decompress from the stress of daily living.

Whoever thought that life in the wilderness would be relaxing was clearly not in their right mind. Every day was full of tasks like waste disposal, farming or security. Though they all agreed it was better than living in Crestwood Hills. That neighborhood had turned into a death trap. They had swung by there only once since leaving and found Mack's home in shambles. Someone had entered and sprayed all manner of obscenities over the walls in red paint and smashed up what furniture remained. Fortunately Bridget didn't see it otherwise she would have flipped.

Brody tossed his backpack down and rolled onto the hammock, he placed two hands behind his head and closed his eyes hoping to get a few hours in. He was exhausted. He was still reliving that moment on the roof and playing back in his head what Chase and Marlin had said. *Was it completely foolish to drop his guard?*

Slowly but surely he drifted off. How long he remained asleep was unknown.

"Hey you!" A soft voice came from his left waking him. Pulling back the large rug that blocked off his corner of the room, Isabel Rodriguez entered. Gone was her police uniform and in its place was a pair of thigh-hugging jeans and a white shirt that hung loosely, exposing the dark T-shirt beneath it. Brody gave a nod then closed his eyes. As much as he enjoyed her company he wasn't in any mood for some long-winded conversation.

"So…" she said. He knew he wasn't going to get any peace.

"Guessing you heard?"

"Yeah, Marlin was flapping his gums. You okay?"

She pulled up a stool and ran her fingers across his neck where there was still a red mark from the noose. "Nah, I feel like an idiot."

She didn't reply but he looked and could see she was nodding slowly.

"They mean well, Brody. We're all trying to figure this out. It's hard to cut ourselves off from the world at large." She exhaled. "I know I've been finding it difficult."

"But I should have known better."

She placed her hand on his chest. "You have a good heart, Brody Slater, perhaps too good. You see the best in people." She shrugged. "It's just unfortunate that things are the way they are."

She eased her way over, slipping into the hammock beside him. He smiled. Over the past four months they had become close. Without her own daughter she had taken Ava under her wing and treated her like her own. She had a way of helping him not to sweat the small stuff. She laid her head against his chest and he ran his fingers across her arm. Her feet tangled up around his and her warm hand ran down his stomach.

"On a good note, we managed to find more batteries, ammo and candy bars."

She laughed and tapped his stomach a few times.

"You want to…" she said making a gesture with her fingers.

He smiled. "And get interrupted?"

She glanced up and was about to say something when Daniel's voice could be heard shouting. "We got visitors!"

They looked at each other. How could anyone have found this place? It was hidden away. No one had been out here in four months. No hunters, no hikers and certainly not anyone from Crestwood. They had made a point of not telling anyone.

"They are armed."

Both of them slipped out of the hammock and grabbed up their rifles and headed out to face whatever threat was at their door.

Chapter 4

Questions swirled around in his mind. How did they find this place? Who were they? Were they related to Malcolm? Brody's pulse raced a million beats a minute. Kai and Todd were already positioned on top of the rocky bluff with their rifles angled down. By the time Brody crossed over to the letterbox, Dolman was exiting the camp. Brody followed after him and came out into the thicket of woods to find two men. They had their rifles swung over their backs and didn't appear to be acting hostile. They were rugged in appearance; one was six foot, the other a little over five seven. Both were kitted out in combat gear, and their skin had a weathered appearance as if they had sat out in the sun for too long. The tallest had a burn mark on the left side of his cheek.

"We aren't here to cause trouble, we just want to speak."

Brody squinted. One of them looked familiar but

he couldn't place him.

Dolman kept his Glock low but ready if they tried anything. He motioned for Marlin and Daniel to move in and disarm them.

"Get on the floor."

"Listen, we just want to talk."

"We do the talking, you do the listening. Now where are you from?"

"Mammoth Lakes."

"Any others with you?"

Brody scanned the tree line and moved out cautiously in preparation for a gunfight.

"It's just us. We came alone."

Dolman motioned to Rodriguez, Gus and Chase to fan out and check the surrounding area. If there were others they were going to have a hard time getting in. The camp was built up on a steep incline, much like old castles. The rocky bluff acted like an impenetrable wall. There were only a few ways in. Through the letterbox; over the top of the boulders, which were virtually impossible to scale unless someone had climbing gear; and the other was by trekking around to the north side, and that would involve climbing. Mack had carefully planned out the location. According to Bridget, he'd spent several months scouting through the outback looking for the best spot, and only then did he seek out the owner.

"What's your business?"

"Cyrus wanted us to speak to you."

Dolman shrugged. "Who's that?"

One of the men eyed Brody and then it dawned on him where he'd seen him before. He would have raised his rifle fast but he wanted to hear them out. The one with the burn mark spoke.

"There are North Korean and Russian troops in Bishop, they have taken residents into custody and are executing anyone who resists."

"Military?"

He nodded. They looked at each other as if trying to grasp what he was saying and decide whether it was true. They had brought up the topic of foreign troops invading but after four months of silence they assumed that the attack on America was just that — a nuclear attack, nothing more — an attempt at crippling the U.S. infrastructure and causing untold deaths without setting foot on American soil. But if this was true, if they were trying to occupy parts of the United States, it would make sense that they would eventually sweep through the smaller towns. They would be easier to control. Once concentration camps were set up, it wouldn't take them long to use the lives of prisoners as leverage to take over what little remained of government.

"And why are you telling us?" Marlin asked pushing the barrel of his gun into the short guy's temple.

"It won't be long before Mammoth is next, Cyrus wants your help."

"Why?" Marlin said skeptically.

"Look, that's all we were told to tell you. He wants to meet this evening."

Brody went over and crouched down beside him. "You haven't told us how you knew we were here."

"We didn't know. Since seeing the troops, we've been scouting out the areas around Mammoth, keeping tabs on those who get close. We initially went to Crestwood Hills and someone told us there that you had all left and gone off to the mountains. We figured you might be accessing it via Highway 395 so we kept a lookout, while a few of us headed into the state forest to check for any signs of tire tracks or campfires. We heard your vehicle."

"Well you can go back and tell Cyrus to fuck himself. Do you honestly think we are that stupid that we would meet up with him?"

"Brody, you know him?" Dolman asked.

Without even turning to address his question, he answered it while keeping a good eye on the two men. "Yeah. The day I headed over to Atomic Jim's place, him and his goons blocked the vehicle. They also attacked us several weeks later."

"You killed several of our friends."

"Because they attacked us," Brody said in a raised

voice. "Now you get up and get the hell out of here. Tell him if we see his face or yours around here again, we won't ask questions."

The men scrambled to their feet and began backing up. Marlin fired a few rounds at the ground and they double-timed it out of there with a look of fear on their faces.

"We should have just killed them," Chase said.

"That's what I was just about to say," Marlin piped up. "Now they'll probably bring the rest of their crew this way." He shook his head and brushed past Brody. He did it in a manner that made it clear he was frustrated.

"You got a problem?" Brody asked.

Marlin jerked his head to one side. "Nope. But I think you do."

"What's that supposed to mean?"

Marlin shook his head and walked off.

"You got something to say, Marlin?" Brody asked.

Dolman walked over and placed a hand on his chest. "Just let it go."

But Brody couldn't. He shouted after Marlin. "So we kill them, who then sends the message back?"

"That is the message," Marlin hollered back without even turning around.

Brody turned and Chase was staring at him. "Go ahead, Chase. Say what you're gonna say. Seems you all think I've lost my thirst for blood."

"It's not that, Brody."

"No? Because you all seem pretty content in killing anyone that we come across. But I try to take a different approach and you act as though I'm insane."

"Well back in..."

"Don't even say it," Brody snapped before walking off into the forest. Ava followed him and he turned around and told her to go back. She stood there looking helpless like a pup unsure of what it was doing wrong. He glanced back over his shoulder one last time to see Rodriguez wrapping an arm around her shoulder and leading her back into the camp. He wasn't sure what was causing him so much internal frustration, the way the country had spiraled down or the lack of empathy. He understood the need to kill anyone who was deemed a threat but if that was the case, why didn't they shoot everyone in Crestwood Hills? As they sure as hell were bordering on being a threat. Why didn't they kill Daniel and his sister when they met them? Or Gus? Whether they wanted to admit it or not, each of them had a moral compass and yet it seemed lately they hadn't been paying much attention to it.

Was it so bad to try and establish connections with new people? Of course, there would always be the assholes who thought that the only way to survive in an apocalypse was to kill everyone that got close. But those folks were the kind that would have been diagnosed with mental problems back when the country was stable. The kind of people that wouldn't stay alive because a day would come when they needed help and no one would be there to offer a hand.

Brody swung his rifle around his back and pulled out a golden tin of cigars. They were small and he'd had them on him since Mammoth. There were only six left and he usually kept them for special occasions but he was pissed and needed to relax. He cupped his hand and lit one with a match, and then pushed his way through the brush until he reached a steep outcropping of rock that looked down over the valley. A hard wind blew against his cheeks, and he gazed at the snow-capped mountains in the distance.

He took a seat on the ledge, and looked off towards Mammoth. There was something about the expressions on the men's faces that made him believe them. He brought down his sunglasses to protect his eyes from the glare of the sun and leaned back on the warm rock and blew out smoke rings into the air. Around him he could hear the sound of the forest, the wind blowing against the trees making them rustle like rushing water.

He hadn't been sitting there for longer than ten minutes when he heard the sound of a branch cracking, like boots pressing down on fallen debris. He twisted over and gazed into the forest.

"Ava?"

He thought for a second that she had doubled back to find him. It wouldn't have been the first time. Except this time no one responded. His hand slid down to the Glock and he pulled it. His movements were slow but purposeful as he raked the tree line with the barrel. Must have been a critter, he thought. Satisfied, he holstered the weapon and returned to gazing up at the blue sky and soaking in the rays. It was sunny but cold.

As his mind dulled, and he found himself drifting off, he didn't hear the man approach from behind. Perhaps he removed his boots? But he felt the sting of the barrel as it smashed against the side of his skull. He let out a groan and went to turn when he was struck again. This time he felt darkness rapidly closing in on his peripheral vision.

"Sorry, but he was adamant that he needed to speak with you."

Those were the final words he heard as his mind went to black.

* * *

Freezing cold water splashed against his face, and he gasped. His skull throbbed, and a faint light stabbed the back of his eyes. Brody came to inside what looked like someone's backyard. There was a shed off to his left, a concrete fountain that had no running water and a garden arbor with several Adirondack chairs nearby. He shook his head and tried to get up but groaned. His mind was in a fog, and his throat dry.

"Steady, you took quite a knock to the head."

That voice. A flood of memories came back in. The outcropping, someone approaching, two sharp jabs to the side of his head. As his eyelids fluttered, several people came into view around him. Instinctively he went for his sidearm but it was gone.

"Yeah," he said slowly. "I had to remove that. You'll get it back. I just need to talk. The name is Cyrus Ramsey, and you are?"

"In pain," Brody muttered through gritted teeth.

The world began to come into view and as it did he

saw the familiar gaunt face, sunken eyes, long hair and beard. He was perched on a low wall. Either side of him were the two men that had visited them up in the mountains.

"Oh, you'll have to excuse the manners of Victor and Joe but they didn't have much choice. Now I've got to ask. Why would you send them on their way without at least hearing them out?"

Brody was glad to see that his hands and ankles weren't tied. He kind of figured they would have restrained him. The man leaned forward and offered him a cigarette. Brody waved him off. He staggered to his feet and then took in the sight of the home.

"Where am I?"

"Mammoth." He turned to one of his men. "Joe, go get the ice pack."

"Ice?" Brody asked bringing a hand up to his head.

Cyrus gave a wry smile. "The perks of generators."

A guy similar looking to him, but with stubble and a slight limp, ambled away.

"So do you do this to everyone you want to talk to?"

"Only the stubborn ones. Now what's your name?"

"Brody. Are you going to kill me?"

He let out a short laugh. "No, Brody. Actually, that would be counter-productive." He hopped down off the wall and brought over one of the Adirondack chairs. "Sit. Take a load off."

Brody rubbed the back of his neck, and head. He glared at the tall guy with the burn on his face before he plunked himself into a chair. Joe returned and handed over an ice pack and a couple of Tylenol. Brody laid the cool ice against the side of his head. It soothed the pain. He could already feel the bulge.

"Now I'll be honest. As you strike me as a man who doesn't like to screw around. Personally it's not my way to reach out to anyone beyond family or close friends but the way I see it, what we are facing right now goes beyond any personal disputes that we have. So that whole thing with you killing several of my friends, I'm gonna let it slide."

"How noble of you," Brody said in a joking manner while leaning forward and wincing every few seconds. He was still seeing stars, and his vision wasn't exactly clear. He continued, "You are aware the reason we stopped that day was to see if your pal was okay, right? I mean, what would you have done if someone turned on you with a machete?"

"Noted. Anyway, differences aside, I figure we have less than twenty-four hours before they push north to Mammoth Lakes, which means we need as many people as we can find who are willing to fight."

"Ask the people of Mammoth."

"Yeah... that's a little tricky."

Brody snorted. "Why don't you just up and leave? Seems more logical to me."

"And go where? If they are pushing east, nowhere is safe. No, I'm not going to be pushed out of my own town. I grew up here. Four generations of my family have lived in these parts and I'll be dammed if I'm going to have some foreign pricks force us out, or worse — place us in custody."

Brody pulled off the ice pack as it was starting to give him brain freeze. "So you intend to face off against an army?"

"No, I intend to strategically take them out one at a time. With help from you of course, and your friends."

"Well best of luck convincing them. Trust me, they aren't into potlucks or fondues. They won't listen to you."

He smirked. "No. That's true. But you," he pointed his bony finger at Brody. "Now they would listen to you."

Brody started laughing for a few seconds but stopped after feeling more pain in his head. "I'm the last person they would listen to, heck, you'll probably have better luck than I will."

"And why is that?"

"Because if they had their way, your two guys would be dead by now."

"So I have you to thank for that?"

"Don't thank me. I'm starting to think I should have shot them."

He glared at the tall man with a look of disdain.

Cyrus leaned forward and shook his finger in front of Brody's face. "I don't think you understand the gravity of the situation. Perhaps I'm going about this the wrong way. Let me show you."

Chapter 5

Bishop was considered a city even though it had less than four thousand people. Brody piled into a Jeep along with six other guys and they took him south on Highway 395 until the turnoff for Sawmill Road.

"How many of you are there?" Brody asked as the Jeep rumbled down an old dirt road, and then veered off across a farmer's field. It was a bumpy ride. Soil kicked up the sides of the Jeep, and they bounced in their seats.

"Eleven."

"So why bother? Why not just get the hell out of here while you can?"

It seemed more logical to run than to try and tackle trained soldiers. It was one thing to deal with roaming gangs, another to go up against the military. They weren't trained for that and they certainly didn't have enough firepower.

"Because my family is in there," Cyrus replied. He

was sitting in the front with his feet up on the dashboard. By all accounts he didn't look like a family man, more the type of individual that would have ended up locked up for pushing drugs or pimping women out. He was disheveled-looking before the apocalypse. Now he fit right in. Everyone had tired eyes with dark circles and bags beneath them. It came with the territory of expecting to be attacked at any minute.

"But you're from Mammoth, aren't you?"

"I live in Mammoth, my parents live in Bishop, so do Joe's."

"Look, I understand wanting to help them but there is a point where this kind of stuff needs to be handled by the military."

"Do you see any of our boys?" Cyrus said. "No, neither do I. They aren't coming. If these troops have made it this far, whatever defenses we had on the East and West Coast are probably crippled. No, this is down to us."

"Here's the thing. The people in my group aren't

going to want to risk their necks when we can remain hidden in the mountains. Troops aren't going to head up there unless they are looking to do a bit of camping."

Cyrus turned abruptly. "You think this is funny?"

"Well, you either laugh or you cry when faced with these kind of situations. I've always had the mindset—"

"Shut the hell up," one of the men said in the back of the Jeep. Brody turned to see it was the same guy that had pummeled him with the rifle.

"Victor," Cyrus said, admonishing him before turning back to Brody. "You'll have to forgive Victor, it was his cousin that you killed that day on the street."

Brody cast a glance over his shoulder and could see him sneering. He was going to make a sarcastic remark about him but chose to remain silent.

"Are we nearly there?" Brody asked.

"We're getting close. We can't go the regular route as they have created checkpoints on the main arteries into Bishop."

* * *

87

Chase had become concerned. It had been three hours since he'd seen Brody wander off into the forest alone. Usually if they were planning to be out that long, someone went with them and they were hunting but after the last conversation, he was beginning to get a sick feeling in his gut.

"Where you going?" Todd asked as Chase headed towards the letterbox.

"I'll be back in twenty."

He didn't want to worry the others. They were already on edge over the visit from the two strangers. The camp's location was compromised and even though it was fairly secure, they all knew what that meant — an attack could be imminent. It didn't help matters that conversation was now swirling around whether the two men were telling the truth. If foreign troops were occupying the United States and setting up labor camps, it changed everything. No longer would they be able to come and go as they pleased. They would have to remain vigilant and possibly even create a secondary camp.

"Brody!" Chase called out as he cradled his rifle and ambled through the forest. Since the fight in Bodie, since losing his daughters and wife, it had changed him. It had changed all of them. Some might have said they justified their decisions and actions too much, and they might have been right but they had learned in a short span of time that one wrong decision could send them down a path and affect the lives of many. They had to be careful. It was easy to react and think later, but every reaction had consequences.

"Brody, I swear if you are screwing around, I'm gonna kick your ass."

As Chase pushed through the brush, heading towards the overlook that they had often sat on to chat about the future of the group, he spotted several of Brody's personal belongings. The tin of cigars was on the ground, laid open, several of them scattered around as if it had dropped. "Brody!" he shouted louder and went over to the edge and looked down. Had he fallen? Jumped? It wouldn't have been the first time they had seen someone take their life. He'd been acting different as of late. Chase shook his head. No, he wouldn't leave Ava behind.

As he crouched down to collect the case and cigars, he spotted gunmetal out the corner of his eyes. Slipped under the cover of sagebrush was his Glock. Now he was concerned. There was no way he would have left that there. He scooped it up and double-timed it back to the camp to let the others know.

* * *

Damon, Cyrus's right-hand man, or whipping boy had parked the Jeep behind a cluster of trees. They had hiked up to a rise that looked down into the town of Bishop. The sun was beginning to wane but from where they were positioned, it gave them a clear shot of the city. All of them got down on their bellies. Cyrus handed the binoculars over and Brody took a look.

He couldn't peel his eyes away. It was hard to fathom that this was their reality now. The North Korean and Russian flags had been plastered in different areas of the city. Jeeps and trucks moved back and forth down the streets on the west side of Bishop. Lines of residents were up against the walls being guarded or frisked. A man trying to prevent them taking his daughter was swiftly dealt with. A soldier stepped forward and slammed the butt of his rifle into his stomach and his knees buckled. Two jabs to the face and he was out cold. The sound of screams carried on the wind as young mothers were separated from their kids. Elderly were piled into the back of trucks and driven away. Where? Who knew? He could only see a sliver of the town from their vantage point. Bishop was spread out with the main street on the east side, and several businesses dotted along Highway 395 that ran through the town until it connected with Highway 6. Brody witnessed a man being shot in the head after he tried fighting back. He pulled the binoculars away from his eyes and handed them back.

"I've seen enough."

"Now you understand why we need to do something."

"I understand that we are at a disadvantage. We are

outnumbered. They have more weapons. If your plan is to go in there and get your family out, you're going alone, as it's a suicide mission. They have that place as secure as Fort Knox." Brody got up to his feet.

"It's challenging. I will give you that but it's not impossible. Brody, with more of us, we can fight back."

"It won't fly with my group," Brody said beginning to walk away. That's when he felt a hand grasp his arm.

"Don't turn your back on him."

He recognized the voice of Victor before he even reacted. Without even a second to think about whether or not they would kill him, he turned and cracked him on the jaw with a left hook. Victor was a large man but the punch was hard enough to wobble his legs and stun him. He would have followed through with a kick to the nuts but Joe and another man they called Damon dived on him and hauled him back.

"Motherfu—"

Cyrus stepped in to intervene before things got out of control.

"I'll kill you," Victor said.

"You'll do nothing," Cyrus said holding him back. "Now go blow off some steam. I need to talk with Brody."

"We are done talking," Brody replied. Cyrus waited for Victor to walk away rubbing his jaw before he turned back. His demeanor had changed. Gone was the tactful guy that was hoping to appeal to Brody's good nature. He charged over and grabbed Brody around the neck.

"I can drop you right here and now and no one would ever know. Now you might not grasp the gravity of the situation that is before us but you will show some respect while you are among us."

His grasp tightened and Brody could feel his windpipe closing up before he released him.

"You are either with us, or against us. You decide."

His eyes flitted across his face, studying him. He understood his predicament. Of course he was going to agree. They would kill him and leave him out among the sagebrush for the birds to peck at his carcass if he said otherwise.

Brody rubbed his neck, which was now raw. He was breathing hard and nothing would have given him more pleasure than to kill the lot of them but he had to reel in his emotions.

"All I'm saying is that I can't guarantee they will agree."

Cyrus leaned forward and pushed a finger into his chest. "Well you better make them agree otherwise the war will come to you."

He didn't need to clarify what he meant, Brody understood. They knew where they were in the mountains. If Cyrus didn't attack, what was to stop them from alerting the foreign troops to their whereabouts? The additional weapons and food they were stocking at the camp would certainly provide leverage.

As they trudged back across hard soil, a strong wind blew in and with it came the sound of soldiers' voices.

"Get down," Brody said, dropping to a knee.

Off in the distance where they had parked, a patrol

of five soldiers had located their vehicle. They were talking among themselves, a mixture of Korean and Russian.

"The checkpoint on 395 was farther up this time," Damon said. "They must have seen us pull off."

"Unlucky for them," Cyrus muttered, rising to his feet and pressing forward at a crouch. The landscape around them didn't exactly offer the best coverage. The Jeep was parked close to Millpond Recreation Area on the far right side and they were hiking across Birch Creek, and land that was nothing more than dirt and sagebrush. They moved quickly and tried to make it to the back of Millpond Equestrian Center. Surrounding it were other smaller buildings, mostly factories and warehouses.

"We need to reach them before they see us, otherwise they are going to radio back and we are going to have one hell of a rough day," Damon added. Brody gestured to Cyrus to take Victor and Joe around the right side of the building, while they went to the left. It was going to be bloody and brutal, but they had few options.

As far as they were all concerned, in that moment, disagreements fell to the wayside and the only enemy was the soldiers before them.

Brody was the first one to take a shot, he honed in on his target using the rifle Cyrus had given to him. He brought the scope to his eye and squeezed off a round. The soldier flopped to the ground and chaos erupted. Quickly they moved forward in combat intervals, obliterating them before they could even react. However, what they didn't know was the sound of gunfire had been heard by two more soldiers who were waiting farther down the road. A Jeep came barreling down and swerved into view. Multiple shots were fired before they gunned the engine and tore away.

"Quick!" Cyrus hollered as they raced towards their Jeep and piled in. Damon was in the process of snatching up weapons and ammo off the fallen soldiers. "Hurry!" he bellowed again. It wasn't as much matter of escaping as it was getting to the two soldiers before they made it out of Sawmill Road and alerted the checkpoint on 395.

There had only been a few times Brody had been in a vehicle where the driver didn't ease off the gas. Once was with Mack when he wanted to scare the shit out of them at the age of fifteen, and teach them advanced driving, and the other was with Marlin in Lee Vining, a town that was under the control of a mad group of individuals.

"They're getting away."

"Like fuck they are," Damon said before reaching into the back of the Jeep and pulling out a rocket launcher from beneath a thick green tarp.

"Where the hell did you get that?" Cyrus said.

Even Cyrus wasn't aware of what his men were up to. Damon didn't reply, he turned and flipped up the sight. "Keep it steady," he yelled as he tried to get a bead on the vehicle ahead that was swerving erratically. No doubt they had seen what he was up to and were shitting themselves. "I said keep it steady."

"Yeah, you try. These roads are terrible."

There was a loud whoosh as the rocket shot out. It

was almost deafening. Within seconds it exploded, kicking up dirt but missing its target.

"Shit!"

Brody brought up the AR-15 and unleashed a flurry of rounds but it was useless. They were too far ahead and within a matter of minutes they would be on Highway 395 and they would escape.

"Can't this thing go any faster?" Cyrus yelled in anger, slamming his hand against the dashboard.

"I've got the pedal to the floor," Joe replied. The roar of the engine, the sight of them escaping made Brody's heart pound in his chest. The Jeep ahead tore out of the road and onto 395. It veered right heading toward Bishop just as they were getting close to the T-junction themselves.

Damon fired off a few more rounds but the distance was too great.

"Go left. Let's get out of here," Cyrus hollered. Brody looked back over his shoulder at the Koreans' Jeep as it disappeared out of view, leaving behind it a plume of grit and dust. If they didn't know they were there, they did now. It would only be a matter of time before they would send out a unit to come looking for them. Mammoth would fall under their control, and more good people would die.

"What now?" Joe asked, the wind whipping through his hair as the Jeep barreled north towards Mammoth.

"That depends, doesn't it, Brody?" Cyrus said tossing him a menacing sideways glance.

Chapter 6

Westbury surveyed the carnage in the small town of Topaz Lake. It was twenty-five minutes outside of Gardnerville, but the journey had taken them longer as they had to shift vehicles out of the way to get through. They wouldn't have stopped or even known that troops had passed this way, had it not been for a mother holding her dead child in the middle of the road. The body of the baby was covered in blood, he'd died in the arms of his father as they and many others tried to escape the foreign troops.

The fair-haired woman pointed in the direction of the Topaz Lodge and Casino, a large wood-paneled building that once catered to the thrills of locals and those in the surrounding area. Now it had been turned into a morgue. Hundreds of bodies were draped over one another as if they had been lined up in a row and gunned down without mercy.

His men kept watch by the doors, and several remained with the vehicle while the rest checked to see if there were any survivors. Though their orders were to protect civilians, the need was overwhelming. From what they had seen in Carson City, the troops were gathering up citizens and carting them away to labor camps, and killing any that resisted. Westbury shook his head in disbelief.

"The rooms are cleared, Sarge," Brooks replied coming out from the back area. They were about to turn to head out when Rocco jogged in.

"Sarge, you are going to want to see this."

"If it's like this, no I don't."

He felt acid come up into his mouth. He'd seen a lot of death overseas but nothing quite like this. It was mass genocide. These were good American people. They didn't deserve this. They followed Rocco out, and he led them down a steep incline away from the building. He led them towards Topaz Landing and Marina RV Park. It was located right on the edge of Topaz Lake. Nearby, streams bubbled and though it seemed tranquil, it was far from it. Laying face first in the dirt was a single Korean soldier.

"Fan out, check the surrounding area for others."

His men jogged away while he crouched down. Rocco jabbed him in the leg and the soldier groaned. "Asshole's alive. Barely."

Westbury approached him slowly, noticing his arms were beneath him.

Both looked either side and saw blood trickling away from the man. Cautiously he turned him over and that's when he took in the grisly sight. Both of his eyes had been removed, nothing but the socket entrails were hanging out.

Rocco backed up. "Fuck!" Repulsed by the sight and smell, Westbury placed a hand over his mouth. The soldier's uniform was open and carved across his bare chest was the word BITCH. Someone had gone to great lengths to torture him and then left him to bleed out within inches of the water. His knees and ankles had been smashed to prevent him from getting up. Behind his body was a trail in the earth where he'd dragged himself through the brush and sand trying to get to the water.

"Sarge! We got more over here."

"Rocco, stay with him."

"Why me?"

Westbury rolled his eyes and moved at a quick pace over to where Castillo was. There were two more soldiers, these had been strung up over posts and had been hung by their ankles and turned into human piñatas. Their faces were beaten to a pulp, the damage was so bad, if it was a crime scene, investigators wouldn't have been able to ID them. Teeth were scattered like small sugar cubes, and below their heads was a puddle of blood. He touched it. It was cold.

He exhaled hard. "What the fuck happened here?"

"You think some of these folks could have been on the trucks that were carted out of Carson City? Maybe they fought back once they reached this town."

It was possible. On September 11, the passengers of

Flight 93 fought back. Though they died, it was believed they saved many lives in the process. Had this been the case here? The trouble was, there appeared to be less Koreans than civilians dead, and no trucks nearby which meant they had to have continued on their journey south. Were they joining up with another unit? The same unit that had butchered Griffin and Vaughn's platoon?

"This took some time," Brooks muttered while cradling his rifle. "They must have grabbed some of the soldiers and held them until the others left. Though I can't see their comrades leaving them behind."

"Depends how hard civilians fought back. Makes you wonder what's going on around the country."

"God, I hope our people are giving them heck. Fuck these assholes," Castillo said before plowing his rifle into the gut of the dead soldier hanging before him.

"More over here. Four have been shot," Martinez hollered.

Westbury returned to the one that was still alive. Though he was in an awful state and barely clinging to life, and probably unable to speak English, he had to see what he could get out of him. With anger boiling over he grabbed a hold of the man and began bellowing at him.

"Where are they headed? Where are your men?"

All that came from his lips was garbled words. He released his grip on his collar and felt around in his pockets and pulled out a wallet. Inside were a few credit cards, some money and a photo of him and what appeared to be a mother and two children. He glanced at the man who would never see them again. It could have been him lying there bleeding out in some hot, humid country. That was the nature of the work they did. There was no guarantee of coming home. He could have done anything with his life; become an engineer, an electrician or a worker in one of the many factories like his old man but he chose to enlist. He chose to sign away his life on the dotted line. Even now faced with what was before them, if he knew this was going to happen, he still would have signed up in a heartbeat. Not everyone was meant to be a soldier but he was.

He rose and pulled his firearm. A single shot into the man's head quickly put him out of his misery. He would have wanted the same. Regardless of his loyalty to his country, Westbury was still human and even the enemy were just doing what their country wanted.

"Let's head out."

He wiped blood from his hands as they retreated to the trucks. As hard it was to see what they had, it meant that the United States was capable of fighting back. It didn't take much to turn the tide, and though the government was standing on shaky ground, his faith was in the people of the country. The ordinary. The brave. The defiant.

* * *

"Enough!" Dolman yelled. "We will have order."

Returning to the camp that evening wasn't easy. Brody felt sick to his stomach at the thought of their reactions. But this was bigger than them now. They couldn't just stand back and do nothing. Despite the previous run-ins with Cyrus and his men, or the fact that it was Cyrus's family that was in jeopardy, this was a matter of fighting for control of their country.

When they gathered around the fire that night, Brody had told them what had taken place and each of them had their own views on what should be done. Marlin was all gung-ho to go down and kill Cyrus and his group, while Chase couldn't believe that Brody even listened to them. Then there was Todd, who was ready to fight.

"Well there you go, I told you the Chinese weren't involved," Kai said with a grin on his face.

"That's still up for debate," Chase muttered.

Kat tossed a stick into the fire and it hissed.

"Just hear him out," Dolman said. "They could have killed him but they didn't."

"It's pretty obvious why they didn't. They need a man on the inside."

"What's that supposed to mean?" Brody spat back.

"You know, Trojan horse style. They are expecting you to feed them intel so they can swoop in and steal what we have."

Brody shook his head. "Some days I wonder if you have got a brain."

"What did you say?" Marlin bolted upright from a log and Dolman quickly intervened.

"Calm down. There is no use getting at each other's throats or pointing fingers. What matters now is what we decide to do from here. Did you see how many troops there were?"

"No, the city is too spread out."

"Seems like an odd place to set up camp, don't you think?" Todd said. "Mammoth has over nine thousand people, well, it did before the black rain. But my point is Bishop has barely half of that. Why there?"

"Honestly I don't think it matters. Who's to say they are staying there? Perhaps they are working their way through the towns gathering people up to take them to specific concentration camps."

Marlin lost his temper and threw a rock. "Bastards. Labor camps in our own country. The nerve of those assholes."

"I can't imagine there are many people there after the black rain," Bridget said.

Gus and Harvey observed but said minimal. They were laying on their sides on top of the outcropping of rock looking out into the forest, every now and again they would look their way and voice their complaints about different ideas that bubbled up.

"All I can tell you is that doing nothing isn't an option. We stay here, they will eventually find us."

"No one knows we are here except your asshole buddies," Marlin said.

"Enough, Marlin," Chase said.

Brody stood up and walked over to Marlin. Dolman and Chase tried to get between them but he reassured them he wasn't going to lay a hand on him. "You think I give a shit about them?"

"Well you helped them."

"I had no choice. It was either work with them or I would have died out there."

"Either way. Your mental state concerns me." He pulled a cigarette and lit it. It glowed in the darkness.

"Mental state?"

He blew some of the smoke purposefully in Brody's face. "You wanted to bring two killers back here. Now you want us to work with Cyrus?" He pointed his finger. "I think you have a few screws loose!"

Brody saw red, and threw a jab. Marlin anticipated it and ducked to his side and came across with a blow to the side of Brody's face. It shook him but didn't drop him.

"Guys!"

The others tried to get between them but it was pointless. Brody was on him fast, tackling him to the floor and plowing his fist into his ribs and following through with an elbow to the face. Dolman and Chase had to drag him off Marlin, a task that wasn't easy. He jammed his heel into the side of Brody's thigh just as Dolman yanked him back.

"Enough!"

Chase stood between them with his hands out as if he was trying to stop traffic coming from both directions. Above, Gus was laughing hard. "God, I love this place."

"Reminds me of when I was a youngster," Harvey said. "Man, I remember having a temper like that."

He turned back towards the forest and squinted. "Guys. Guys! We got company."

Marlin was up faster than anyone else. Thankfully, Todd had removed his rifle and put it out of reach while they were fighting. Rodriguez went over to the letterbox and peered through the foliage.

"Who is it?" she called out to Harvey. A few flashlights flicked on from above and then a great deal of yelling occurred.

"Stay right where you are. Don't move." He shouted down. "There are at least eleven of them, maybe twelve."

"Eleven," a voice called out from over the boulders.

"It's Cyrus," Brody said, wiping his bloody lip. He was crouched over nursing the cut. Everyone exchanged confused stares.

"You brought them here?" Marlin barked before trying to lunge at Brody again. He wasn't fast enough, Brody pulled out his Glock and held it right up to his forehead.

"Whoa, Brody," Chase said. He wasn't about to shoot him, but he was just tired of Marlin's outbursts. He held it there for a few seconds before pulling it away and heading over to where Rodriguez was, to give her a hand taking away the rocks blocking the entrance.

"And there we go. Letting them in. I told you he was going to be the death of us."

Of course they took precautions. Dolman wouldn't let them inside unless their weapons were confiscated. Cyrus was more than willing to do that. As he passed by Brody he smirked. "I see what you mean now. Tough crowd."

Once they were inside the camp, they circled around the fire and Cyrus spoke up.

"Well if you don't mind I'll skip the introductions.

By the looks of it, our good friend here appears to have done that already ."

"Friend, see," Marlin muttered loud enough that Brody could hear.

"As you are aware, this situation had reached a code red. Now you can stay up here and play Little House on the Prairie or work with us to push these assholes out."

"Work with you? Why would we work with you?" Marlin asked.

"Don't make us out to be the bad guys here. What we did in Mammoth was no different than what all of you have done since this has kicked off. It's a matter of survival. It's not personal."

"Firing a gun at me is," Marlin said.

"Ignore him, he just enjoys arguing," Brody said touching a cold cloth that Rodriguez had got for his bottom lip. If looks could kill, Marlin's could have buried him as he was throwing some serious daggers.

"Look, I can appreciate your reluctance. We don't exactly have a good history."

"You think?"

"But we are all residents of this town, all Americans and that has got to count for something. We are not asking you to do this for us. Do it for yourself. Do it for your country."

Marlin scoffed and shook his head. "How long did it take for you to come up with that line? Seriously you should submit that to the Marine Corps, perhaps they'll use it in their next recruitment video."

"Very funny." There was silence then Cyrus continued. "We've killed some of their men, so you can be sure they are going to come looking for us. Who knows, maybe they are already in Mammoth, killing other innocents. People you know. People you lived and worked beside. If we work together perhaps we can drive them out."

"By the sounds of it, there are too many to go up against," Chase said.

Brody chimed in. "We might not be able to tackle them head-on but we can certainly make things difficult for them."

"He's right," Cyrus said. "We're not asking you to agree tonight. But think about it. Just don't think on it too long. It's only a matter of time before they find you here. Hell if we could, they sure as hell can."

He began heading towards the letterbox. Cyrus gestured to the others in his group and they followed him out.

"Where are you going?" Brody asked.

"Back outside, is that okay? The atmosphere in here is a little too uptight for my liking."

Brody glanced over at Marlin and narrowed his gaze. Before the night was over they would need to make a decision. Perhaps Cyrus's approach to getting help was completely ass backwards but if the situation was reversed and it was any one of their families down there, they may have done the same. A big challenge awaited them, but if they all worked together the odds of surviving were better than if they didn't.

Chapter 7

War is messy. No one in their right mind would willingly go if they had another choice. Of course there would always be the patriots, the ones who saw it as a badge of honor. The kind of guys who enjoyed cracking heads together, grunting and pulling at their nuts as a display of manly bravery, but that was all bullshit, nothing more than male egos run amok.

After Cyrus and his group exited the camp, they remained outside creating a smaller camp a short distance away. Even after they parted ways, the discussion on what should or shouldn't be done continued. It wasn't getting them anywhere. The group was divided on what to do. Half were convinced that aligning with Cyrus was absurd, the others didn't it see it that way. They felt it had nothing to do with Cyrus. It was a matter of principles. If your country comes under attack, what are you supposed to do? Flee? Hide? Or fight?

"We can go back and forth on this all night. The way I see it we put this to a vote. Those in favor of fighting, raise a hand."

Eight hands rose.

Marlin snorted. "Well I guess that answers your question. We have women and children to think about now, Brody."

"Is it really that, Marlin? Or is this your way of sticking your heels in the mud?"

"Fuck you."

He strolled off. Brody turned to Dolman. Dolman had been one of the ones ready to fight, though his wife and daughter weren't keen. Protection was in his blood. Cops were proactive. They didn't wait until it was safe to charge ahead. They ran into buildings when others were running the other way. It went beyond duty.

He shrugged and grabbed a hold of Brody's shoulder. "You know I would be there with you if I could but we agreed that for this to work, we all have to be in agreement."

Brody nodded and glanced at Chase. Chase had been one of the ones who didn't raise his hand. He'd sided with Marlin, though Brody was sure that was because he was worried about Matt. Matt on the other hand had been eager to fight. That kid had nerves of steel.

As Brody went to bring the news of the decision to Cyrus, Ava took a hold of his hand. He was going to tell her to head back but instead he took her with him. Over the past four months he'd spent a great deal of time with his daughter. Mostly getting to know her and discovering what he'd missed out on. Though the situation had been difficult, that was the one good thing that had come out of the attack on America — It had drawn him and his daughter back together and given them a chance at rebuilding what his bitch of an ex had forced apart.

Brody swept the flashlight over the trees as they trudged through the dense forest heading in the direction of a small fire further down.

"Dad, you aren't going to fight, are you?"

He glanced down at her and shook his head. "No."

She'd been concerned about losing him since that fateful day in Bodie. It was part of the reason why she followed him wherever he went. She'd become like his shadow. To her, he was the only sense of security that she had in her life. The one sure thing.

"Ah, Brody, finally. Please tell me you have good news?" Cyrus asked.

They were seated on logs around the fire, warming their hands when he came into the clearing.

"Look. Cyrus."

"Actually, hold that thought. Don't tell me. Take a seat. Join us for a drink. I think I," he paused to correct himself, "we, misjudged you. Watching you go out on a limb with your people speaks volumes about you. The way you handled yourself back there with those soldiers. I'm guessing you've had some training."

"I wouldn't say it was much of anything."

"Maybe not, but you didn't hesitate. You knew what to do and took command of the situation. Those are valuable attributes in a war."

Brody cleared his throat and was about to share when Cyrus rose and came over. He placed a hand on his back and led him over to a space near him.

"Is this your daughter?"

Brody nodded.

"Beautiful girl." He motioned to Damon to give him a drink. A bottle of bourbon was passed around and handed to Cyrus. He poured some into a metal cup and handed it to him.

"And what might your name be?" he said hunching over.

"Ava."

"Ava. Well you know your old man here is something else."

Brody got a sense that Cyrus was attempting to butter him up. It was pointless. The group had made a decision and there was no going back on that. The way they saw it, there was currently no one in danger and no one was willing to lose their lives over Cyrus's family. Sure, there was a risk in staying where they were but it was so off the beaten path and miles from any town or city, the chances of the troops finding them were next to none. And even though he disagreed with the decision, he wasn't crazy enough to go by himself or stupid enough to think that Cyrus wouldn't stab him in the back the first chance he got. At the end of the day, they had killed some of their people. The deaths of friends and family members were never taken lightly. He knew that Cyrus was just biding his time until they were back in a position of power.

Cyrus motioned to one of the women in his group. "Lucy. You want to get Ava a drink, maybe something to eat?" He turned back to her. "You hungry, sweetie?"

"She's already eaten," Brody said.

Cyrus smiled. "Ah but what does that mean nowadays? Kids are always hungry. What about a treat?" He turned back to Lucy who had brought over a can of Coke and a Mars. "Huh, what about that?"

Ava's eyes lit up but instead of taking it she glanced at Brody, waiting to see if he would approve. What was he going to do, say no? He gave a nod and she took it and thanked him for it. Cyrus beamed as if he was some contestant on a game show.

He exhaled hard. "These are precarious times we are living in. No doubt about that." He reached into his pocket and pulled out a box of Cuban cigars. He flipped the lid and extended one to Brody. Brody took it and Cyrus drew near to the fire, took out a piece of flaming stick and brought it close to his face. Once it was lit, gray smoke filled the air and for a few seconds he felt relaxed and at peace. The fact was they were no different than them. They were looking out for their own interests, protecting their loved ones and trying to survive under crazy conditions.

"You worked at Von's before this, right?"

Small talk, an attempt to bridge a gap. Brody was familiar with it.

"That's right."

Cyrus stared into the fire as he puffed away on the cigar. "Don't the old ways seem meaningless now? I mean, our lives were filled with running here and there trying to keep up with the world around us. Jobs. Kids. Friends. Dreams. And for what?" He flashed him a sideways glance. "In a matter of days it will all be gone. We'll all be buried or end up as the bitch of the Russians and North Koreans. But you know what?"

Brody glanced at him.

"At least when we worked for the man, we got to choose whose bitch we were going to be. Your bitch was some large franchise supermarket. Mine was people who needed their vehicle fixed. But now… we have no choice once they get their hands on us."

He took a hard pull on his drink and blew out more smoke. He never said anything else for a few minutes. It was as if he wanted what he had said to sink in.

"Anyway. Sorry to be a downer but I just think it's clear what we have to do. We either fight or surrender. Eventually they are going to sweep across this country and take control, if they haven't already. At least this way we know we can go out with a little respect. Don't you want your kid to respect you, Brody?"

Brody scoffed and tossed the cigar into the fire.

"Stop it."

"What?"

"The act. You already know the outcome of the decision my group has made. They are not going to help. You are on your own with this. So, this whole act of trying to butter me up is not going to work. I don't agree with their decision but I respect it. And you are going to need to respect that too."

"I don't need to do anything. Let's get that clear right from the get-go."

His tone shifted quickly. Though the fire offered warmth, Brody could feel Cyrus's cold stare on him.

"Tell me, Brody. What are you going to do? Stay here? Hope they don't find you?"

He didn't reply.

"Because they will and when they do, you won't have us to help. Your friends... they are making a big mistake."

"Maybe so. But like you said. We get to choose."

Brody rose from the log and extended his hand to his daughter. She was still tucking into the remaining part of the candy bar. "Come on, Ava."

"Nice meeting you, Ava," Cyrus said before leaning back and studying them both.

She smiled and he tossed her another candy bar. Brody took it and tossed it back at Cyrus.

"Too much of anything isn't good," he replied.

It wasn't that he didn't want her to have it but this was just a game to Cyrus and he wasn't going to have his daughter stuck in the middle of it.

As they walked back to the camp, Ava protested. "I could have had that."

"And rot your teeth? There are no dentists now."

"But that was my choice to make. He gave it to me."

"Until you are of age, I make a lot of the decisions for you."

"Mom would have let me have it."

"Yeah, well your mom is not here to make that call."

Ava stopped walking while Brody continued for a few more steps. He turned back and she tossed the can of Coke at him and raced into the camp, tears flowing down her cheeks.

"Ava. Come on. I didn't mean it that way."

Discussing her mother was a touchy subject. She still was processing the reality, which was her mother wasn't coming back. More than likely she was dead along with her deadbeat boyfriend. He'd tried to have words with her but she just shut down, or ran off. Kids were tough to figure out. One moment he thought he was doing right by her, the next, he was in her bad books. He couldn't win for trying.

When Brody entered the camp Dolman looked to be in good spirits.

"Brody, over here."

He glanced at where Ava had gone and considered

following her but decided to give her some space to calm down.

"What is it?"

"Come, check this out. I've been scanning through the different frequencies trying to see if anyone else is out there. Others, you know, like us."

He led him back to where they had the ham radio set up. Dolman sat down and started fiddling with the knobs and then he handed the headphones to him. There was static coming out of the speakers and then a voice came over the line.

"Do not adjust this frequency. This is a freedom radio broadcast. It will last only sixty seconds. It is the only free voice remaining in the country. If you can hear this, know that the United States is at war and troops are occupying parts of the East and West Coast. The power grid is not completely down. I repeat. It is not completely down. Reports have come in of areas of power from Michigan to Idaho and Louisiana to Utah. Our troops are fighting back but they need your help. I repeat. We are at war. If you can hear this now, we fight for our freedom. Never give up. Never surrender."

Then the line went dead. Nothing but static.

Brody pulled off the headphones. A surge of hope washed over him. He smiled as did Dolman and for a second he placed a hand on his shoulder. "Huh. Well ain't that something!"

Chase had been listening and he chimed in. "Maybe life will go back to normal. Now all we need to do is wait it out. Our boys are coming. They will sort these assholes out."

Brody turned to him and screwed up his face. "Did we hear the same broadcast? They are calling for everyone to fight back."

"Of course, if you come under attack but we are safe here, Brody. My son and baby are safe. Ava is safe. Dolman's family is safe. No one is coming here."

"I can' t believe you still think that? What happened to the guy who was ready to charge headfirst into Malcolm's camp?"

"That was different. I had Matt and Tiffany and the baby to think about."

"And the people of Mammoth?"

Chase's eyes dropped ever so slightly. "They have a choice. Just like us."

Brody shook his head unable to believe what he was hearing.

"There are good people still down there. You didn't see what I saw. Women being shot. Children weeping over their parents. Elderly being dragged like rag dolls and tossed into the back of a truck. Teens lined up and beaten because they protested. What if that was your Matt down there?"

Chase got up and wouldn't look at him. "It's not. And we have made our decision."

Brody grabbed a hold of his arm as he tried to leave. "That's bullshit and you know it."

"Get off, Brody. Now!"

Dolman tried to say something but then chose to remain quiet. Tensions were running high and everyone was entitled to decide what was best for them and their family. It wasn't an easy choice to make. Fighting back against military troops could mean certain death. Chase left the small enclosure leaving only Dolman and Brody standing there.

"Cyrus might be wrong about many things but this, he's not. I'm not going to let the others dictate what I do. You heard it. Americans are fighting back. We need to do the same. I'm going with them. If you want to stay, stay."

"But Brody. We agreed."

Brody ignored him and exited the building to search for Rodriguez. He had a few words to say to her before he headed off. His mind was swirling with the danger that lay ahead. How would they go about this? And was he really ready to lay down his life for America?

Chapter 8

The enemy had left a bloody mess in their wake. By the time they reached Walker, they had seen more than their fair share of Americans dead. They were beginning to think that any chance of catching up with the group that had wreaked havoc was nothing more than a pipe dream. That was until they came across a group of civilians pinned down in the middle of the street behind a cluster of trucks.

They might have continued driving south on Highway 395 if it hadn't been for the noise of gunshots. The armored trucks veered off onto Hackney Drive to find the source.

"Any sign of where that's coming from?"

"It's as black as the ace of spades out there, Sarge."

As the trucks rumbled along the street, Martinez, Jones and Graham were outside of the one truck. They were wearing night vision goggles and carrying suppressed rifles. They fanned out in combat intervals with their rifles cradled as they got closer to the noise of rapid fire.

Brooks brought the truck to a halt and they all piled out.

"Stay alert," Westbury said giving hand gestures and the men moved forward towards a corner. At the corner he could see eight contacts dressed in civilian clothes. They were crunched down and taking a considerable amount of heat from Russian soldiers. There had to have been at least ten of them pressing forward.

Westbury motioned to his team to move in and provide support, while six of them went around the buildings on the left. They were to hold off firing until he gave the signal over the comms. Westbury moved away from the corner, running at a crouch from one vehicle to the next with Parker and Castillo. He tried to get the attention of the civilians but the noise of gunshots was deafening. Fire from vehicles crackled and lit up the street. It was like a war zone in Afghanistan. Many of the buildings had been destroyed and were laying in rubble.

They pressed on trying to get as close as they could without being seen. Parker pulled off a grenade, as did Castillo and they lobbed them over the vehicles past the civilians. There was a tremendous explosion and the Russian soldiers backed up, dragging one of their injured men behind an SUV.

"You think this is the leftovers from Topaz?"

"Possibly."

"Come this way!" he shouted to the four civilians. One of them was nursing an injured leg that they had wrapped up with a T-shirt. It was bloody and the man was unconscious. Two of them scooped him up and hurried towards the soldiers.

"God, are we glad to see you guys," a bald-headed man said before ducking out of view. Bullets continued to snap and ricochet all over the place. Several of his team tossed smoke grenades to try and provide cover. It was a chaotic scene but after what they had gone through in Carson City, this was nothing.

"Any others out there?" Westbury asked.

"Yeah, but we can't get to them. And I think they are dead."

Another one asked, "How many of you are here?"

"Seventeen," Westbury replied.

"That's it?" a woman cried, her face dirtied by smoke and grit.

"Afraid so," Parker replied before squeezing off multiple rounds. Several punched through vehicles, and others took out a Russian who was sneaking up the side of a nearby building.

A man with a thick beard extended his hand. "Dave Summers. I served in the army, eight years."

"Sergeant Westbury. You out of ammo?"

"Yeah," the man said glancing at the Beretta in his hand.

"Around the corner you will find an armored truck, head over there. One of the Marines will give you a rifle."

The survivor patted him on the shoulder and took off while they tried pulling back with the remaining survivors. It was a young mother and a child, along with an elderly man and another man in his late thirties. Castillo went about checking the injured man and using his medical training to help.

"Please tell me our boys aren't all dead," the elderly man said.

Westbury wasn't sure how to reply to that. The country had suffered a tremendous setback. Communications had been down for quite some time before they got word that areas of the United States were still in operation and remaining troops stationed on warships were heading back to provide additional support.

"I don't know the full extent of what's happened. But we are here to protect civilians. That's all I can tell you."

He ducked as bullets continued to rain down. Westbury could see soldiers zigzagging their way forward.

"Parker and Castillo, get the injured out of here. I'm pressing forward."

Across the street, Martinez, Rocco and Jones were

laying down some serious heat. Every few seconds, concrete would fly in the air as grenades erupted. The body of a Russian soldier spun in the air like a rag doll.

Westbury sucked in a breath and pressed forward, unleashing a flurry of rounds. Anxiety swirled in his body as he took in the sight of how many there were. Amid the smoke it looked as if they kept multiplying. Obviously there were more of them, out of view, farther down the street.

He fired off a round and hit one of them in the skull. The guy dropped and one more rolled into view. "Bastards. These fuckers are multiplying."

Over the comms unit he checked in with the six-man team who'd circled around.

"Tucker, you in position?"

"Roger that, Sarge."

"Open fire when ready."

"Roger that."

The beauty of the street they had pulled into was that it had created a funnel into which the troops ahead of them had squeezed themselves. This placed them at a disadvantage. As Tucker and the rest of the team came around the back and began lobbing grenades, Westbury could see the horror on the faces of those bastards as they realized they had been hedged in on either side. As soon as the explosions lit up the place, he popped out and fired off a burst taking two of them down. Jenkins was the closest and had already taken out three of the soldiers when his body buckled.

"Jenkins!"

He hurried over to him and crouched down but it was too late. A bullet had gone straight through his eye. Another kill only fueled his rage. Westbury tossed the magazine, slammed another into place, chambered a round and began opening fire. That's when he noticed what Jenkins was trying to do. Ahead in a parked vehicle was the silhouette of two heads bobbing up and down. Kids. What the hell?

"Jones, Parker, give me some cover."

The noise assaulted his ears as he ran at a crouch

towards the vehicle; he slipped by a truck and saw a dark mass out the corner of his eye. He reacted just in time to see a Russian land on him. Tackled to the ground, he began rolling around with the Russian for a few seconds before he realized the guy had a blade in his hand. Using all his might, he forced his weapon arm back, head-butted him in the face and reached for his sidearm. In an instant the gun went off and the soldier's body went limp. He pushed him off and continued on. When he reached the vehicle and pulled the door open, he could see the kids cowering in the back. They couldn't have been more than ten years of age. Both were sobbing hard. The back window shattered and glass went everywhere. Westbury turned, raked the barrel of his rifle back and forth and unloaded several rounds before grabbing a smoke grenade and tossing it. It would provide a small amount of cover while he got them out.

"You're going to be okay, give me your hand," Westbury said. They shook their heads. Fear prevented them from trusting him. They probably had no idea if he was a good guy or the enemy. "Look," he motioned to his right shoulder where the American flag patch was. "I'm not going to harm you."

He turned again and unloaded a round at the sound of a soldier's boots. Over the comms he shouted, "Parker! Where the hell is my cover? That one was too close for comfort."

"Sorry, Sarge, it's getting a little hot over here."

"Well it's like hell where I am. Get me out of here."

He turned back to the kids. "If you want to live. Let's go!"

With a little hesitancy they reached out and he grabbed their hands and pulled them out. He shielded them with his back as they hurried back towards the cover of where Parker and the others were.

"Holy fuck!" he said as he got around the corner. "Castillo, I need you back here to take these kids out. And the rest of you, let's keep pushing in. We are not leaving here until every single one of them are dead."

* * *

"No. You can't do that, Brody." Rodriguez ran a hand through her hair.

He was quick to reply. "She's become attached to you. You've seen it yourself."

She moved forward and placed her hand on his chest. "She still needs her father. Going down there is only gonna get you killed."

"Waiting here isn't going to help. The only way we are going to survive this is to fight. No more justifying our actions. No more hiding away. Before, we had a reason to stay out of sight, there was no threat at our door but now there is. I need to know that you are going to look after her if I don't make it back."

Rodriguez shook her head, her eyes welled up but she turned her head to hide her face. Brody moved closer and took a hold of her chin and brought her around so he could see her eyes.

"What about us?" she said.

He arched his eyebrows. "Us? I didn't..."

"You didn't think about that."

"No, I didn't know there was an us."

She huffed and stepped back placing some distance between them.

"I didn't mean it like that. I just thought we were taking it slowly. You know it's only been four months. And..."

"You thought you could just play with my emotions and then walk away, is that it?"

Oh God, this was not going the way he saw it playing out. He thought he would tell her to look after Ava and he would head off with a kiss. Nope. He'd dug himself an emotional grave, and she was tossing him in it. He exhaled hard and backed away from her. He didn't need this now. Not now. He already had enough on his plate with the thought of how Ava was going to react.

"I can't promise you anything, Isabel. Not now. I..." He was about to say something when she cut him off.

"Just go. I'll look after her."

"Isabel."

She turned away and walked off without saying another word. It wasn't the outcome he was hoping for but there was no time for trying to explain. Either she understood or she didn't. As he came out of the cabin, he paused at the door and looked at the rest of the group who were milling around by the fire. Daniel and his sister walked into one of the other cabins and Marlin let out a laugh while talking with Chase. He could stay but that wasn't going to be of benefit to anyone except themselves.

He went over to the ammo and rifle area, unlocked the door and gathered up more ammo. Then he donned a bulletproof vest, snatched up some night vision goggles and crossed over to where Ava was staying. When he entered her room, he looked around at the wood-paneled walls. She had covered them with pieces of 8x11 paper tacked on the wall with pins. Some of them were drawings of people's faces from the camp, others were of a darker nature and depicted soldiers fighting. She was laying in her hammock reading a book when he entered. He dropped his bag and she noticed it.

"You're going with them, aren't you?"

He sighed and pulled up a small stool. "I know you don't understand it now but one day you will, Ava."

"I knew it. I knew you were going to leave me alone. You're just like mom."

"Ava."

She tossed the book across the room and turned on her side. He placed a hand on her shoulder and she tried to shake it off. He could hear her sobbing gently.

"Ava, if I don't go do this, there is a chance that men are going to come and separate us anyway."

"But at least you won't be dead."

"Maybe not."

He didn't know what to tell her. Nothing he could say would make it right. A kid just wanted a parent to be there. She'd already been through enough with the divorce but staying back and doing nothing was out of the question. He couldn't do that.

"Isabel will keep an eye on you. I love you, Ava." He leaned in and gave her a kiss on the side of her face and then left before she convinced him to stay. Outside in the corridor he wiped a tear from the corner of his eye and then forced down his emotions. As he came out and headed towards the letterbox, Todd joined him carrying a rifle.

"What are you doing?"

"Going with you."

"But you voted to stay."

"That I did. But I changed my mind."

"There he goes, the big hero," Marlin said, letting out a laugh before chugging back on another beer. He was three sheets to the wind, so Brody ignored him. Todd wasn't the only one that had decided to go, Gus slid down off the rock and told him to hold up.

"You should stay, Gus."

"What, and leave all the commie bastards and North Koreans to you two? Like hell, I have wanted to get back at them since the cold war."

They trudged on into the night, only briefly looking back. Chase stood at the entrance of the camp watching them. He said nothing and he didn't change his mind but deep down, Brody knew he was contemplating going.

As they made their way down to the clearing, Cyrus and the others had already packed up their gear and were getting ready to head out. He smiled and one of his eyebrows arched. "So you changed your mind."

"Not for you."

"I didn't think so. Good. Three. Not exactly what I hoped for but we'll take it."

He gave them a hand getting their gear together.

"How did your daughter take the news?" Cyrus asked.

"Let's get something clear before we leave. I don't like you. I don't intend to like you. The only reason I am here is because of the way Americans are being treated in Bishop. Once this is over, if we survive, we are going our separate ways. So anything you need to ask me, it had better be related to the mission at hand, as that's the only time you are going to get a response from me. Do I make myself clear?"

Cyrus narrowed his eyes and pursed his lips, he sniffed hard before saying, "Crystal."

Chapter 9

Enemy troops were everywhere. Cyrus's initial plan was to cut through Mammoth, head south parallel to Highway 395 to avoid any soldiers who may have gone north to locate them. That plan went out the window when they reached the outskirts of the town. Positioning themselves in a cluster of trees overlooking Main Street, they could see soldiers dragging out people from their homes. It was brutal. Every now and again they could hear gunfire. Though they couldn't see everything that was going on, they knew people were being killed.

"Well that rules out heading down Main Street," Todd said.

"It rules out a lot."

"Nothing's changed," Cyrus said, peering through night vision binoculars. "It was to be expected. We just kicked a hornet's nest by killing those soldiers near Bishop."

"So what is your plan?" Brody asked. He was curious about what he had in mind being as he hadn't mentioned anything since leaving.

"Plan? My plan is to kill these motherfuckers."

"That's it?"

He shrugged. "That and get to my family."

"I thought you had given this a bit more thought than that. Tactically I mean."

Cyrus lowered the binoculars and cut him a glance. "Stop busting my chops and get down there with the others."

"And what about you?"

"Someone has to keep watch over their movements."

"How about I do that?" Gus said.

"Old man, you barely look like you can tell the time on your watch."

Gus gritted his teeth and glanced at Brody. He figured he was giving Cyrus one pass, the next time might be different. Brody, Todd and Gus didn't move.

"Okay. Okay. You want a plan. Here's one, we kill them and steal what technology they brought with them. It might give us some strategic insight into how they are operating. Does that satisfy you?"

Brody was beginning to regret going with him. He was an arrogant prick.

"I say we observe them. Watch what they are up to, and plan out a course of action. But tonight is not a good time to attack."

"Really? You came all the way down here to turn back now?" Cyrus said. "There are fourteen of us. More than enough to take out that squad."

"We don't know how many are down there. Charging in there would be suicide."

"Charging in there is why we came."

"No it's not. It was to get your parents out of Bishop. There are ways to do that while reducing casualties. I say we come back in the morning."

"The morning? They might have shipped off my family by then. No. It happens tonight."

"Then you are going to have to do this alone," Brody said getting up and preparing to walk away.

"Cowards."

Brody spun around. "This isn't about being a coward. It's about using some fucking common sense. Tell me. How many do you see right now?"

Cyrus just stared back at him, so he repeated.

"How many?"

Cyrus looked through the binoculars. "Fourteen."

"That's what you can see on this stretch of road, but what about Minaret or farther down? Do you really want to take the risk of racing in there and getting us all killed?"

"You must have known we were going to encounter this."

"Bishop. Yes. But not here."

"How's this any different?" Cyrus got up from the ground and walked over to him. "We would have been faced with the same in Bishop. In fact there would have been far more soldiers." He stared blankly at him. "Oh...

you thought we were on some reconnaissance mission. Just observation?" Cyrus scoffed. "Now I get it. You had no intention of engaging with them."

"That's not true," Brody replied. His eyes darted to the others who were fanned out along a ridge that overlooked a section of Main Street. Down below fires burned out of control. Several screams could be heard through the rumble of engines.

"Or maybe you have cold feet? Is that it?" He looked at Gus and Todd. "And what about you two? Are you both pulling out?"

It was a mixture of several things. None of them were soldiers, and even though they had fought a fight in Bodie, and faced off against multiple threats since then, it was different to fighting in a war. Mack's voice echoed in his mind. *You can go in with the best of plans but things can go belly-up in a matter of seconds.*

"The problem is not that we don't want to fight. We don't want to fight without a plan of action. Your idea is to go charging in and hope to God that there aren't a dozen more troops around the corner. But what if there are? What then? By the time you figure out what to do, they will have called in reinforcements and I don't know about you but I don't like the idea of fourteen against fifty or more trained soldiers."

Brody turned to walk away.

"Then their blood is on your hands."

He paused for a second, balling his hands.

"The only reason you won't go down there is because you don't have a reason to. Now if it had been your kid, your wife or your friends, things would be different. Wouldn't it?" Cyrus snapped.

Brody remained rigid, looking off into the darkness of the night. Cyrus was right to some degree. The potential loss of family and friends would motivate anyone to take greater risks, but for strangers?" He heard another woman's cry. It grated at his heart. Even though they were Americans, people he had lived beside, that didn't change anything. Without a plan, it was suicide.

"You know what, Cyrus. I don't give a shit what

you think. I came down here to help because you told us you had a plan of action. Now, I can tell that you just had a death wish."

Cyrus stared at him blankly. He was about to speak when Damon came rushing up. He'd gone off to scout out the town with three others. Brody figured he wouldn't return.

"Cyrus, there are only sixteen of them."

He smiled at Brody. "See. I do have a plan. We know how many there are now. You want to leave? Feel free. But if you do, you're a coward."

He jogged away with Damon. Damon gave a confused look but continued down the steep incline that would lead out of a section of woods. They would then have to cross multiple roads and pass through the yards of houses to reach the main stretch. Brody tapped his foot a few times contemplating what to do.

"We don't have to do this," Todd said. "Let him go and get himself killed. We can turn back."

The word coward continued to play in his head. He

wasn't easily baited into an argument by what people said. Years of working with the public had forced him to get a grip on his emotions but there was something about Cyrus that riled him up.

"I'm going in. I'll understand if you guys want to go back."

He started edging his way down the steep incline, several branches scraped his face. He stumbled a little, but managed to steady himself against a tree trunk. He flipped down the night vision goggles he'd brought along and everything took on a green hue.

Ahead of him he saw Cyrus look back, and he swore he saw him grin. What the hell was he doing aligning himself with a lunatic? Dirt fell away from beneath his feet and he nearly slipped as he came down the final section that brought him out onto Forest Trail. He ran at a hunch across the road and raced into the next section of trees.

His eyes continued to dart from side to side looking for threats. His pulse was racing and though he was mindful that he could lose his life, something about what they were doing felt right. The words from the broadcast echoed in his mind. *Never surrender.* Someone had to fight back against this enemy. Maybe they couldn't win the war but they could put up one hell of a fight and drive back the enemy in towns all over the United States. How many others were out there doing the same thing? The very thought boosted his morale. They weren't alone. Behind him he could hear the sound of Gus and Todd. He swept his gun back and forth taking in his surroundings. At least Ava was safe. That's all that mattered. No matter what happened to him, he knew Rodriguez would take care of her.

A cold wind blew through the trees like an invisible enemy trying to force them back, or cause them to second-guess. Above them a thick blanket of dark clouds blocked out what should have been a beautiful sky full of stars. Beyond the sounds of screams and rounds being fired in the distance he could hear Cyrus instructing those around him to fan out. The area before them was filled with juniper trees and pinyon pines. These year-round trees provided much needed cover for what lay ahead.

They crossed Alpine Crescent and pushed on through the backyards of multiple homes. Without anyone to tend to the yards, it had all overgrown and now the grass was knee high, and filled with weeds and all manner of plants. Mother Nature had consumed the area, covering up every inch of concrete on the ground with creeping vines.

As they drew closer to Viewpoint Condominiums, he could see six soldiers, they were hauling surviving citizens into the back of a truck and barking at anyone who moved too slow.

Some of them were carrying K2 assault rifles, others K3 machine guns. They were kitted out in green camouflage combat gear and were shooting anyone who protested. Brody caught up with Cyrus and they took a knee beside a large pine and gazed out at the chaos unfolding.

"Joe, take Ruby and Victor and be sure to cover us

from the left. Damon, take Maddox and Sadie, cover the right. Aiden, you are coming with me and Brody. Let's hit them fast, move in and grab the weapons and ammo. Don't hesitate."

They all nodded and moved into position. Each of them raised their rifle and from the cover of the tree line squeezed off suppressed rounds. Soldiers dropped like flies while Mammoth residents ducked and put their hands over their heads. They had no idea who was firing or if they would get caught up in the crossfire.

As more soldiers saw their comrades fall, all hell broke loose and rounds began chewing up the tree trunks in the forest as they returned fire. Todd yanked a grenade, pulled the pin and threw it as hard as he could towards two soldiers who had taken cover behind their truck. It hit the ground and rolled beneath. The front end of the truck lifted above the explosion, sending the two men back ten feet.

"Careful. We want at least one of those trucks," Cyrus yelled as he ran forward into the clearing and unloaded multiple shots in rapid succession. In a matter of minutes they had taken out eight of the sixteen. The sudden attack overwhelmed and confused the Koreans. It was unexpected and violent.

Brody raced in and grabbed hold of a woman and her daughter and told her to run for the tree line. He twisted around, just in time to see Aiden get shot. He landed on his face and wasn't moving. They pulled back behind the truck that had exploded and was now on fire and tried to take cover from the remaining eight soldiers.

"We don't have long. They will be calling for backup and who knows where the backup is," Brody yelled. He darted out and unleashed a flurry of shots before dropping and rolling behind a battered SUV that was providing cover to four guys in their late teens. By the looks on their faces, they were petrified. One of them had already pissed himself with fear.

"Listen up, stay behind me. We're getting you out."

A black kid grabbed Brody's arm. "Man, there is a lot more than this."

Brody turned to him for a second, his face screwed up. "What?"

"When they arrived, we saw four trucks of soldiers. This is only one," the kid said.

"Shit!" Brody said. He knew it. There was no way in hell the Koreans were going to send in only sixteen men. They were combing through the town rounding up as many civilians as they could. All of which meant they were close by, probably farther down on Main Street or one of the adjacent roads. How many more? They could be looking at forty plus soldiers.

The noise of gunfire was deafening. Without any communication device he had no way of telling Cyrus or the others who were pressing forward with little regard for what was coming.

Brody pulled a smoke grenade and lobbed it out to provide additional cover. The smoke drifted across the road like a ghostly apparition.

"Okay, move out," he yelled, holding one arm back to keep them from stepping forward into the line of fire.

He unleashed more rounds and pulled back. The boys ran at full tilt, keeping their heads low. With so many rounds being fired, it was impossible to protect them from the assault. One of the boys was struck in the back and collapsed. His friend rushed to his aid but realizing there was nothing he could do, scrambled away, tears pouring down his face. Was it his friend or brother? Death had no preference. Before the night was out, they would see many more die at the hands of the enemy.

Once the other two were out of harm's way, Brody darted through the heavily wooded area, burst out across the next road and slid down an embankment to reach Cyrus who was pinned down behind Mammoth Brewing Company. Not far from there in the parking lot was a mound of bodies. Brody took in the sight and couldn't believe it. Many of the bodies were slung into commercial dumpsters like garbage. Pools of blood bathed the parking lot. Each of the green industrial-sized dumpsters was overflowing with the dead. They had massacred fifty, maybe seventy people. What the hell? It felt like the wind had been knocked out of him. For a second he didn't even realize that he was lingering in the clearing while coming under heavy fire. Snapping out of the shock, he rushed forward and slid on the ground, tearing his pant leg. He scrambled to get behind a wall.

"There are more," Brody bellowed.

"What?" Cyrus yelled back over the noise of gunfire while returning fire.

"Koreans. Three more trucks coming. We need to pull out now."

"I'm not pulling out. We are taking these out, retrieving the weapons and ammo and one of the trucks and then heading for Bishop."

Brody grabbed hold of him. "Listen up, you stubborn sonofabitch, we are not dying tonight. For once in your life listen to someone else. Civilians confirmed it."

Nearby, several grenades exploded and sent hot shrapnel in every direction. Dust and concrete filled the air. Off to his left he could see Gus taking position behind a Chevy truck. He pulled up his rifle and laid it on top of the hood, brought his eye up to the scope and squeezed off two rounds. The remaining eight soldiers were taken out over the course of the next ten minutes. For a brief moment, Brody thought they were going to escape but then they heard the rumble of trucks approaching from behind, to their left and right.

Chapter 10

There was no time to escape. One truck was coming south down Minaret Road, the other two from the east and west on Main Street. Thinking fast, Brody scanned the area and honed in on the dumpsters full of the dead.

"Shit!" Cyrus said, pulling out a magazine, slapping in a new one and chambering a round. "These motherfuckers want a war, I'm going to give it to them."

Brody grabbed him by the wrist. "No. Follow me."

"What?"

Brody got up and started double-timing it over to the large industrial dumpsters. "Come on."

Cyrus's hesitation didn't last long. He shouted to the others and they sprinted across the parking lot. "Get in!" Brody shouted, making a waving motion with his hand. One by one they climbed in and hid themselves beneath the mountain of bodies. Brody was the last one in, he dropped into the bloodbath full of limbs, smeared his face with sticky blood, and piled a body on top of him. Inside it smelled rancid, a mixture of iron, grime and human waste.

From beyond the steel container, he could hear trucks getting closer, and then Koreans yelling as boots pounded the pavement. Multiple shots were fired. All the pain he was feeling in his thigh had been replaced by a rush of adrenaline. To his left he could see Cyrus staring at him, not moving a muscle. He didn't trust him. That hadn't changed. But in that moment, he pushed his differences aside to focus on making sure that neither of them died.

He couldn't understand a word the Koreans were saying but it was clear they were fuming. It must have burned them to know that their entire unit had been wiped out before they could return to help.

The sound of boots got closer to the dumpsters. Brody closed his eyes and held his breath, praying in his mind for them to walk away. One of them must have peered inside as he heard his body slap up against the metal siding.

More yelling ensued, though this time Brody heard an American's voice, a familiar sound — it was Gus. His eyes widened in horror. Then came the sound of a match being lit, and the aroma of a cigarette. He went to move but Cyrus reached over and placed his hand over his mouth and shook his head.

"You sons of bitches, you can go to hell for all I care," Gus cried.

They could hear Gus being beaten. His groans, and the sound of someone assaulting him ferociously made Brody sick to his stomach. How didn't he spot him? He just assumed everyone was nearby. What about Todd? He didn't even think about him. The Korean soldier that was nearby walked away. The sound of his boots crunching gravel grew faint. Brody desperately wanted to sit up and look over the edge but Cyrus was holding him in place.

They were torturing Gus. No doubt trying to get information out of him as to who had killed their comrades but he wasn't saying a word. He just kept replying with the words *fuck you*. Then one single shot rang out, and it was over.

Brody squeezed his eyes shut and balled his fists. Rage swelled inside him. More yelling and then the trucks' engines roared and the vehicles moved away. They stayed inside that dumpster for what felt like half an hour before any of them made a move. It was Damon appearing at the lip of the dumpster that caused them to get out.

"It's all clear."

Brody pushed his way out from under heavy arms and climbed over the top. His eyes scanned the parking lot and fell upon Gus. His body was slumped to one side, a single shot to the temple. Brody staggered over to him and dropped down onto his knees, looking at him. He swallowed hard and took a moment to let it sink in that he was gone. Here was a man who had courageously fought alongside them when he didn't need to.

"We need to go, Brody."

"Where?"

"Bishop," Cyrus said.

"No. I'm not going yet. I'm burying him."

"It doesn't matter."

"It does!" Brody yelled back and glared at him. "He was a friend." Brody ran a hand over his tired and bloody face. He wasn't sure if it was blood from his thigh or from the dumpster bodies. He remained there for a few seconds until he felt a hand on his shoulder. Brody turned to see Todd. He was safe, covered in blood but alive.

"I'll give you a hand. We'll take him back."

He nodded and slowly but surely they hauled up the body of Gus and began making their way out of the lot.

"Others are going to die, Brody."

"Not tonight they aren't," he replied as they continued on. He didn't care if Cyrus went on to Bishop by himself. It was late, close to two in the morning and he was tired and emotionally drained.

The journey back to Iron Mountain was filled with

silence. A few times he heard Cyrus speaking with Damon but it was just to ask for water or a cigarette. Even Cyrus knew it was madness to attempt to attack Bishop after what they'd just been through. They needed to regroup, bury Gus and rethink. All of them could have lost their lives that night.

* * *

By the time Sergeant Westbury and his team made it to Bridgeport they were all exhausted. They had fought hard for several hours in Walker, taking back control from the Russian patrol that had massacred countless Americans.

As much as he wanted to press on, his men were tired, besides Griffin and Vaughn had made it clear they would be fine until morning. They were concealed and would remain there until the platoon arrived the next day.

Several of the men had got out to clear the road ahead of vehicles that had been positioned to prevent entry to Bridgeport. They were cautious as they went about removing the battered vehicles. With every town that they came across on their way down, they had to remain on alert. Westbury sent out Parker and Jones to scout out ahead. Once they had the vehicles moved out of the way, they brought the truck around the back of the Bridgeport Inn, covered it with camo netting and headed inside to get rest for the night.

"Bring in the MRE's, Graham."

"Yes sir."

On the outside, the place wasn't much to look at. White clapboard siding with signs that read: bar, breakfast, lunch and dinner. Inside it was decorated in shabby-looking wallpaper from the '80s and the place had a pungent smell to it like hobos had taken up residence or dogs had been in and taken a shit.

Graham handed off an MRE to him and he told three of them to keep watch. The others would get their heads down for an hour or two before they would rotate. Westbury entered one of the rooms and slammed the door behind him. He breathed in deeply and slumped down on the single bed with solid oak headboard and footboard. On the wall was a picture of Abraham Lincoln. It was strange. Almost out of place. Below it was a quote from him that read: *Those who deny freedom to others deserve it not for themselves.*

He snorted. Out of all the towns they decided to stay in, all the inns and rooms, he ended up in the one with a quote from one of the greatest presidents of all time. What a fuck-up it had been with the latest president. It didn't matter who got into power, they always screwed it up. People praised them on the way in, and tore them down the very next day. That's why he never bothered voting. It was just a game, a means of giving people some sense that they were in control. No one was in control. Oh, but how government liked to make people believe they were. If they only knew.

He slumped down on the bed and went about eating the slop out of the MRE bag. It was beef stroganoff. Westbury stared at the wall thinking about his family and if he would see them again. But it wasn't his own that he was concerned about the most, it was the family of Jenkins. He was a good man, a fine soldier and he'd met his young family. He was just at the beginning of his career. Certainly dying with his boots on was something every soldier was prepared to do. But if given the choice, he knew that even the most diehard soldiers would rather live than gain a medal of bravery that they would never know about.

After downing the godawful food he got up and went over to the small mini bar and popped it open. It was bare. Of course it was. Alcohol had become like gold now. He pulled out a cigar and lit it and crossed the room to the window. Outside, he could barely see anything except the silhouette of a few buildings and stalled vehicles. It was hard to imagine it had been four months since the USA had been attacked. He knew the American people were probably wondering where the military were. They were out there going from town to town helping as many as they could but with so much of America crippled it was hard to operate on the scale they would have, had they managed to contain the threat before it happened.

There was a knock at the door. "Come in," he said without turning around.

"Sir. The boys thought you might want some of this."

He turned to find Jones holding a small bottle of Jack Daniel's. That was one thing he could count on with his men, they weren't selfish. The bond he'd formed with the soldiers in his platoon had been forged through fire and blood. All of them would have given their lives for each other.

Westbury took it and didn't ask him where he got it. It didn't matter.

"Take a load off, Jones." Gary Jones was one of the most recent soldiers to join his platoon. Up to now he hadn't had the chance to get to know him, they had only been on one tour overseas together and in that time he was nose deep in administration and the day-to-day challenges that faced the troops in the east.

Westbury walked over to the side table and scooped up two glasses that would have been used for water at one time. They didn't look very clean but then nothing about the hotel was sanitary. He poured out two fingers of golden liquid and handed him one.

"You got family, Jones?"

"A daughter, sir. Six months old."

"Shit. I remember that age."

"You have kids, sir?"

"One. An eleven-year-old boy named Dustin. A good kid."

"Things still good with your old lady?"

"She can be a bit of a handful but we remain on good terms."

Jones stared down into his drink, holding the glass with both hands before knocking it back.

"Sir, you think we'll make it out of this?"

He glanced up at the image of Lincoln. "Who knows if our commander in chief is still alive? Knowing him, he's probably sealed away in some bunker praying that we are dealing with the problem."

"And we are."

He turned back to him. That's what he liked about new recruits. They had this go-get-'em attitude. They acted like they were invincible. A few more years and he would soon change his tune. They all did. The military had a way of changing a man. For some it brought out the best, for others the worst. It wasn't just what they witnessed while on tour: the death of young children, the carnage of a nation and the atrocities of mankind. It was what they didn't see. The country helping them. But maybe now they would. He couldn't get out of his head what he'd seen back at Topaz Lake. America was fighting back. Even if they had been crippled. The nation wasn't going to go down without a fight.

* * *

Brody stared at the mound of dirt. His hands as well as his knees were covered in soil from having dug the grave. Now they stood around Gus's body wrapped in a sheet. He helped Dolman lower him into the hole and cover it. Though Cyrus and his crew wanted to be there for the funeral, Marlin and Chase wouldn't let them back in. They had written them off as nothing but trouble. He could see the anger in their faces when they returned carrying Gus's body.

Dolman shared a few words and there was a moment of silence before the group thinned out and went their own way.

"I knew this would happen," Marlin said, still gazing down at the mound.

"He made his own choice."

"But he wouldn't have gone if you hadn't."

"Not everyone is going to see life like you, Marlin. Gus might have died tonight but I don't think for one minute he regretted coming along. The man had courage."

Marlin screwed up his face. "What, and we don't? Is that what you're saying?"

"About time you stop acting so defensive," Todd added.

"Shut up, Todd," Marlin said not taking his eyes of Brody for even a second. "So let me guess, you are going out again in the morning, aren't you?"

Brody shrugged and then locked onto his gaze. Marlin stepped forward and grabbed a hold of his arm. "How many more have to die before you stop?"

"Stop? We are at war, Marlin. You weren't down there tonight. You didn't have to pull yourself out from beneath an ocean of dead bodies, or haul a friend back up a mountain."

"No I didn't and neither would you if you hadn't got a God complex."

"And by that you mean?"

"I think you know."

For a moment Brody was going to let it slide. He knew Marlin was just baiting him into another argument. An argument that wouldn't go anywhere but as much as he tried to hold his tongue he couldn't. He snapped. Brody yanked out his Glock from his holster as Marlin had his back to him. He rushed over and grabbed him by the back of the collar and placed the barrel against the side of his temple.

"How's that feel, huh? You like that?"

Dolman was across the camp when he saw it all taking place. Chase tried to intervene but Brody wouldn't let him go. "No. You need to wake up. As the next time you feel a gun against your head, it's going to be the enemy's."

He pushed away and strolled back to his cabin leaving them wondering what had just happened.

Chapter 11

Brody didn't sleep much that night. He was up at the crack of dawn, standing on a jagged rock watching the rising sun change the morning sky from a dark gray to a deep orange. Spread before him in the valley that led down to Mammoth was a wild river, its frothing waters partially hidden by the pine trees that clustered together near the edge.

He took a hard pull on his cigarette, the smoke swirling upward and mixing with the cool air. Only the sounds of critters in the forest could be heard, along with birds chirping and singing their morning songs. A shimmer of silver caught his eye and he saw a small boat drift downstream. The one occupant didn't appear to be in a hurry. Another survivor who was probably camping in the National Forest, he thought. Behind him, Rodriguez greeted him with a wave and a quick hello before disappearing into a cabin. He acknowledged her with a slight smile. It was the only energy he could summon.

The previous night had taken a lot out of him, and yet at the same time it had boosted his confidence. It was natural to be scared and want to shy away from the heat of battle but there was something to be gained in facing the enemy and making it clear that this was their country and no one was going to push them out.

His head throbbed a little. He needed some coffee. A little bit of caffeine so he could face the day — a day in which he knew Marlin and the others would be arguing once again about why he felt the need to go off and fight. And that was just one of the many challenges ahead of him. He had no idea what Cyrus had planned or if any of them would return.

Before all of this, life in the camp had been smooth sailing. Each of them knew their place. They had got into a routine. Days were filled with hunting, collecting supplies or working on the defenses of the camp, evenings they created their own entertainment, playing cards, reading, chatting or going for long walks into the forest. For months, all of them had felt safe, at least compared to what they had just been through. The mountains offered them security and concealment. A way to start afresh and heal both physically and mentally. Brody knew it wouldn't last. Nothing did.

Rodriguez appeared at his side.

"How did you sleep?"

"I got a few hours," he replied.

She cleared her throat. "About last night..."

"I would prefer not to talk about it."

"Brody. You know they're going to bring it up this morning. Why don't you nip it in the bud and go and apologize to Marlin?"

"For what?"

"For what? You put a gun to his head. That's not like you."

"No, maybe not. But perhaps it's what he needed."

"No one deserves that."

He glanced at her. "Are you questioning my mental

state?"

She shrugged. "I just think that perhaps the recent news of troops invading has put you on edge."

He shook his hand before flicking the remainder of his cigarette to the ground and stubbing it out with his boot. "See, that's the bit I don't get. How is it that I'm the only one here besides a few individuals who sees the danger in us doing nothing?"

"I don't see it that way. I think they just need time for it to sink in. Not everyone is the same when they get bad news. Trust me. In all my time as a cop, I have come across all manner of people. A few years back, I had to deliver news to a mother of a nine-year-old boy who had died in a hit-and-run. You want to know her reaction?"

He didn't respond.

"She was completely blank-faced. She didn't want to come down to the morgue and see her son. There wasn't even a smidgen of emotion conveyed by that woman. Cut forward three weeks. I got a call about a woman who was in distress down at the local café. I walk in and sure enough it's the same woman. Sitting in the corner, sobbing her heart out. Hell, she wouldn't let anyone get near her. She was tossing cups and all manner of shit around. I managed to get her to calm down. You want to know what caused the reaction? She heard a song play on the radio that her son used to play in the house. That was it. One thing triggered it. All the emotion, all the pain inside bubbled to the surface." She paused for a second and adjusted her position on the rock. "Now a month ago, I had almost the identical situation. A son knocked off his bike. The mother broke down in my arms when I told her the news. Two people, exactly the same situation. Each of them responded differently." She glanced at him. "You have to give people time to let things sink in. Just because you are reacting this way and Marlin and Chase aren't, that doesn't mean they are weaker than you, or dumb or even cowards. They just need time to process it in their own way."

"That's the problem, Rodriguez. We don't have time. The wolves are at our door and I wouldn't be surprised if the troops are out there now trying to hunt us down for what we did yesterday. It wasn't a victory as the war is not over but it was a step in the right direction."

"For you. For now. But for others, you can't rush them. Neither can you put a gun to their head. That shit don't fly, even among friends. You're better than that."

Brody exhaled hard. He rolled his head around. He needed that coffee. The nicotine wasn't cutting it. He'd considered quitting altogether and for a while he had until the shit storm of the century brought turmoil into his life. He figured he'd eventually cut back.

"Out of everyone I thought Chase would have understood what needed to be done. He was the first one to want to charge headfirst into Bodie, and yet now, it's like the wind has been taken out of his sails."

"That's because he has Matt and the baby to think about. And you have Ava or have you forgotten?"

He looked at her for a second before glancing out across the valley. "How could I forget? I have spent the better part of her life not involved because of her mother.

As much as I love my kid, my kid isn't going to have a life if I don't fight for the freedom that she deserves. That we deserve."

"But what can be gained if she loses you in the process?"

He shrugged. Was there really an answer for that? Go or stay, there were risks. Why did anyone join the military and go off to war? Did they care so little for their family? Some might have said yes. Brody didn't think that was the case. In his mind, they cared so much for their family that they were willing to face a threat and lay down their life if need be. It's what Mack had taught them about. He'd ingrained it in them. After all this time he thought Chase, Kai and Marlin would have grasped that.

Isabel placed a hand on the small of his back. "Anyway, give it some thought. Now you want to get some coffee?"

"Please," he said stretching out the word.

As they strolled back to the fire pit, others in the camp were beginning to stir. Kai came outside and stretched out. He looked over and gave a salute before heading off to relieve himself. Harvey Crumlin was already awake. He was busy stirring up a pot of coffee. The sweet aroma mixed with the smoke of burnt wood filled Brody's nostrils.

"Morning. I caught some fresh rabbit yesterday, you want some?"

"I'm not sure I can stomach it," Brody said. He wasn't hungry. It was always the same when nerves got the better of him. It wasn't as much the thought of heading down to Bishop and getting embroiled in another battle as it was facing Marlin. He knew what he'd done was wrong. He wasn't thinking straight. He took a seat on a log and Harvey poured into a couple of cups. It was instant coffee, not exactly the best but far from the worst.

"Ava still sleeping?"

"Yeah," Isabel said. "Checked in on her before I came out."

"Was she upset last night?"

Isabel nodded. Bridget emerged from her cabin and

made her way over. Slowly but surely each of them appeared and joined them. Over the past few months, mornings around the fire had always offered each of them a time to talk about their plans for the day but that morning they were quiet, except for Harvey and Isabel. It was to be expected. Losing Gus was more difficult than they thought it would be. In only a short time they had become a close-knit community, and the fact that he wasn't there was only made more evident by his empty chair.

When Marlin poked his head out, he didn't stop at the fire, even though Brody called out to him. He headed towards the letterbox with his rifle and didn't look as if he was in the right frame of mind.

"Marlin!" Brody called out.

"Brody, probably best to give him some space," Dolman said.

"No, I need to get this cleared up and apologize."

He shot off in the direction he was heading. When he caught up with him, Marlin stopped and cast his gaze down at the ground. "What is it?"

"Where you heading?"

"Does it matter?"

"Look…" Brody tried to find the words. "I'm sorry about last night."

"Okay." He turned and began walking away. Brody frowned and fell in step.

"Okay? That's all you're gonna say?"

"Yeah."

"But I put a gun up to your head."

"And? What do you want from me, Brody?"

What was he meant to say to that? "I…" He stumbled over his words and Marlin started to walk away. He made it a few yards when he turned and came charging back jabbing his finger at him.

"You know I used to think that Kurt Donahue had problems, but compared to you…" He scoffed and shook his head.

"I'm sorry, Marlin."

"So what if I make a choice to stay and not fight?

Does that make me any less than you? Is it wrong to want to stay and try and live?" He waited for an answer but Brody didn't give it, so he continued. "I just want things to go back to the way they used to be."

He exhaled hard and shook his head slowly while looking off into the forest.

"I know, bud."

"Brody!"

Brody cast a glance over his shoulder and Kai came running out. "Ava is gone."

"What?"

"Isabel checked her bed a few minutes ago, and it was stuffed with pillows. It doesn't even look as if she slept in it last night."

Not wasting a second, Brody double-timed it up to the camp following Kai into the cabin. He burst into her room and looked around, just wanting to see for himself.

"Did anyone see her leave last night?"

"She was here," Isabel said. "I swear, she was here when you all got back. I tucked her in. I thought she had slept in this morning."

He ran a hand through his hair. "Oh God."

"Does she sleepwalk?"

"Not as far as I know."

"I'll check the cabins," Marlin said.

"I'll head down to the creek," Todd added.

Over the course of the next ten minutes they scoured the camp and the surrounding area, calling out her name. Brody's mind was a mess. The thought that she could have wandered off in the night, perhaps slipped and fallen, plagued him.

"Any luck?" Brody shouted to Dolman who had wandered uphill to see if she had gone to one of the lookouts. She'd always been fond of heading up there as it provided an amazing view of the landscape.

"Nothing."

Then it dawned on him. Had she gone down to Cyrus's camp to get some more candy? He'd seen the way she was around Lucy after they gave her a Coke and a Mars.

"I'm going to see if she's with Cyrus."

"I'll come with you," Marlin said.

And like that, whatever disagreement they had with each other, it fell by the wayside. Their friendship was stronger than misunderstandings and outbursts. As they made their way down through the thick forest, Brody muttered to himself under his breath.

"I shouldn't have gone, or said what I did about her mother."

He was thinking of every reason why she might have run off.

"You think she would have tried to return home?" Marlin asked.

He shrugged as they quickly made their way down the steep incline. "Who knows."

They thought of her heading into Mammoth where the troops were patrolling troubled him greatly. It was his worst fear.

"God. I told her not to do this. You'd think by now she would have learned."

"You don't know, Brody. Ava is a smart kid, I don't think she would have run off without a good reason."

"That's what bothers me."

As they got closer to the clearing where Cyrus and his group had set up camp, his eyes widened. They were gone. There was nothing left except a blackened fire pit that was still smoldering.

"Where the hell are they?"

"Ava!" Marlin yelled. "Did you tell them you were going with them today?"

"Yeah. I think."

"Maybe they assumed you weren't going to leave after what happened to Gus."

He shook his head and frantically searched the immediate area, crying out her name. "I'm going down to Mammoth."

"Wait, Brody. We'll come with you."

The others had caught up. Kai, Todd, Chase and Dolman.

"No. This is my problem. I shouldn't have…"

"Enough, Brody. Your problem is ours too. We are going with you."

Dolman shouted over his shoulder. "Daniel, Harvey, gather together what weapons we have and tactical gear. We'll head out in ten."

With that said he walked over to Brody and placed a hand on his shoulder. "Brody. Brody!" he raised his voice, snapping him out of his tunnel vision. "It's going to be okay. We'll find her."

He waited there while the others got themselves ready. As much as he wanted to leave immediately, the danger ahead was more than he could handle by himself. Tension hung in the air and he was beginning to get antsy.

"Listen, I'll head down. You can catch up."

"No, Brody. They'll be here in a second."

Dolman shouted out again. A few minutes passed and the others returned, this time however Kurt came down as well. He was holding a piece of red cloth, a bandanna, the same kind that Brody had seen Lucy wearing the night before. "Isabel found this in her room." Brody snatched it out of his hands and stared at it for a second or two. Slowly he tightened his grip on it, and gritted his teeth before yelling.

"Cyrus!"

Chapter 12

"Do you see her?" Chase asked as Brody looked through the binoculars. They had positioned themselves in a different area to the night before.

"No, but the place is swarming with Russians and Koreans, even more than last night. Looks like they aren't setting up a camp, just gathering people together and processing them."

"Processing?"

"Sorting through them, separating the elderly from the rest, along with children, women and men." He handed the binoculars to Chase and he took a look. "You see the two trucks at one o'clock?"

He nodded and frowned. "Holy shit. This is insane."

Brody rolled onto his back and looked up at the sky. Anxiety filled his being. A sound could be heard in the distance, like a tremor. It slowly morphed into a roar and then two fighter jets tore through the air. It was bright that morning and it was hard to make out whose they were.

"Were they ours?" Todd said, cupping a hand over his eyes and glancing up into the sky.

"If it was, they aren't here to help us. They are probably heading to Sacramento."

Chase continued to scan the town below for any sign of Cyrus and the others but so far there was nothing. They figured he'd circled around Mammoth and headed for Bishop.

"Why would he take her?" Donahue asked. "He knew you were going to help him. It doesn't make sense."

"If he took her," Brody said, he still wasn't sure but signs were pointing to the fact that Lucy must have slipped into the camp in the night and snatched her up or lured her out. The question was how?

"Who was on the gate last night?"

"Harvey."

He would have asked him if he'd seen anything but

he'd stayed back with the rest of the women to make sure Ava didn't show up. Right now, they were going on a hunch, that was it. Nothing more than a gut feeling. For all they knew, Lucy could have given Ava the bandanna.

"Old fool. He probably fell asleep," Donahue said. "Listen, without knowing where she is, it's probably best that we head back."

"We just got here," Chase said. "No one is going anywhere."

"We've been here for over an hour and you haven't seen squat. And let's face it. The chances of Cyrus attacking are slim to none. He's no Marine. He's probably miles away from here griping about the fact that we didn't help him. Knowing him, he's headed north towards Canada. Something I think we should all consider doing."

"He's right," Daniel said. "Look at them down there. There are way too many for us to go up against and that's just in Mammoth, how many more are in Bishop? This isn't like dealing with ten or twenty."

"And leave them all down there?" Dolman asked shaking his head.

"They had plenty of chances to leave," Donahue said.

Brody turned back over and squinted. "He's down there, I know it. Where though?"

"You think I can take a look?" Marlin said holding his hand out. Chase turned and handed him the binoculars. He cast Brody a glance before looking through. There was silence for a few minutes and then he cursed. "Bastards. I say we take out one of those trucks. See if she's among those who are being driven out."

"And how do you suppose we do that?" Donahue muttered.

"I know this town like the back of my hand. All of us do. Let's use that to our advantage. Here's what I have in mind."

Marlin began to share his idea. It wasn't foolproof but it was possible it could work. The trucks were heading down Main Street until they merged with Highway 203, then it was a clear shot until it reached Highway 395, where they would turn off and go south.

"Between 203 and 395, we have a five-minute window. It gives us a short amount of time to create a momentary distraction."

"Like?"

"Look around you. How many stalled vehicles are on the roads? We roll a few into place, plant some of the C4 in each and light them up when they approach."

Donahue chuckled. "You knucklehead, you want to kill all the civilians? I thought the goal here was to find Brody's daughter not blow her to kingdom come."

"No, you idiot. We're not going to blow it up, we're gonna create a distraction and slip onto the truck. If they're on there, we'll get them off before they even know what's happened."

Donahue arched his eyebrows. "Yeah, that is the most insane plan I have ever heard. But hey, I'm up for it."

Brody just listened while looking up into the sky.

He was going over where Ava may have gone if she had run away.

"Hey guys, check this out," Kai said handing the binoculars to Chase. He peered through and adjusted them.

"Well goddamn. If it isn't Cyrus. Asshole."

"What?" Brody shifted over and tore the binoculars away and took a look. Sure enough Cyrus was down there walking alongside a commanding officer in the Korean army. Either side of them was what appeared to be Russian higher-ups. He didn't look perturbed or concerned and he certainly didn't look as if he was being held against his will. A few minutes after they had come out of a hotel, the rest of Cyrus's group appeared. Frantically he scanned them waiting to see if he could...

His stomach dropped when her face came into view.

Lucy was holding her hand and pulling at it. Ava had tears streaming down her face and was trying to pry her hand loose.

"She's down there." He scrambled up and tried to move forward but Chase grabbed a hold of him.

"Brody. No."

"Ava is down there," he yelled.

"And we'll get her but not that way."

"She's just a kid!" He screamed out loud, his voice smothered by the forest around them. Rage filled his being at the thought of her getting harmed. He brought the binoculars back up to his eyes and watched helplessly as they loaded her onto a truck along with a whole bunch of kids. His eyes darted to Cyrus who looked to be acting very animated and pointing in different directions. *What the hell are you up to?*

"Isn't his own family down there?" Donahue asked.

"Yeah. He's probably doing an exchange."

Donahue muttered. "Adults for a kid?"

Chase looked over at Brody. "Oh no. No. The camp."

He scrambled to his feet and sprinted into the forest.

"Chase."

He waved them off. "Just go, I'll join up with you later."

Daniel went with Chase, while the rest remained and headed east through the forest to try and get to the road that joined onto Highway 395.

"Pick up the pace, they'll be moving them soon."

Six of them, Rodriguez, Dolman, Kai, Marlin, Brody and Donahue, hurried through the thick underbrush, pushing back limbs and darting in and out of the trees while cradling their weapons. Sweat beaded on Brody's forehead as he ran at a full sprint. It was crazy to think it had come to this. A nation invaded, people being rounded up in towns and shipped off to work in labor camps.

When they reached Highway 203, they ran at a hunch towards the road and quickly began setting up a roadblock. All it required was shifting the stalled vehicles into neutral and then pushing them out into place. Kai kept an eye on the road while they moved fast. Once they had them arranged, Marlin pulled off his backpack and went about setting C4 to the underside of each of the vehicles.

"Hurry up, they're coming."

Each of them raced to the ditches either side of the road and slid down the embankment back into the tree line. Brody darted behind a tree and raised his AR-15. There was no telling how things would proceed, it was a gamble but one they had to take. The large truck rumbled as it made its way towards them. There was only one. Marlin sat nearby with the detonator, just waiting for them to stop the vehicle and get out. As it got closer, the driver eased off the gas and stopped a fair distance away from the blockade.

Todd frowned. "What's he doing?"

No one got out of the vehicle.

"Come on. Get out," Marlin said to himself, his finger hovering over the remote detonator. They could see activity on the truck. Several of the soldiers got up and appeared to be talking to the prisoners. A door hissed, and four soldiers stepped out and nervously looked around before slowly making their way up to the vehicles. The driver remained on the bus, shifting back and forth between looking at the passengers and the road ahead.

They shifted their focus towards the tree line and for a moment Brody thought they saw them but the trunks of the trees were wide enough to cover their bodies.

"That's it. That's it, go a little closer. Check it out."

A grin spread across Marlin's face, then he pursed his lips and hit the trigger. Instinctively Brody shielded his eyes with his forearm as metal exploded and shot up into the air in a cloud of dust and fire. When he looked back, the men were nothing more than body parts scattered across the ground.

"Move in!"

The second he said it, the driver slammed the gear into reverse and attempted to back up. Brody dropped to a knee to steady his rifle, and brought the scope up to his eye. The truck swerved as he attempted to pull it around.

In the few seconds that were required to straighten it out, Brody managed to get him directly in his line of sight. He exhaled and squeezed the trigger. A single round shattered the driver's side window and the soldier slumped to one side. The sound of kids screaming could be heard coming from the back as they rushed up to get them out. Donahue flipped down the flap on the back of the truck and one by one they started helping them jump down. Brody scanned the faces waiting for Ava to come into view.

Two, four, six, eight, ten, he was counting them as they came out, when the last one hopped out, his heart sank. She wasn't inside that one. Brody yelled in frustration.

"Guys! We got company," Kai shouted out.

* * *

Doing anything under pressure had never been one of Chase's strengths but add to that running up a steep incline and it was torturous. Matt, baby Rachael, Alisa, Harvey, Christine, Nancy, Bridget, Amanda and Todd's mother Edith. Their names rolled around in his head as he and Daniel scaled the side of the rugged mountain. It was rough terrain and hard to get through even when they were hiking but running was unbearable. They were heading for the bluff where they had stashed the truck, somewhere along the Mammoth Scenic Loop. From there it would be a twenty-five minute drive to the end of Deadman Creek Road, and then they would have to hike from there on out. He knew that if the troops had already made it to the camp, they'd see them on the way back or at least come across one of their vehicles.

Panting hard and out of breath, Chase's lungs burned as he arrived at the truck. They yanked off the camouflage netting and branches concealing it and hopped in. The engine roared to life, he slammed his foot on the gas and tore out of there. He nearly lost control of the truck multiple times as it wound its way up the winding path. His heart thumped in his chest, adrenaline kicking into high gear. Chase drove wild, smashing the accelerator and slamming the brakes when he had to.

Daniel nearly toppled over as they careened through turns. His jaw tensed and then relaxed like a switch being turned on and off. His eyes darted to the rearview mirror and then back at the road ahead. The sun peeked through the trees, and the glare caught him off guard. He squinted and slapped down the visor just so he could see. That twenty-five minute drive was over in a matter of ten minutes. By the time they made it to the end of Deadman Creek Road, his knuckles were white from gripping the steering wheel so tight.

There was no sign of any military vehicles. That was a good thing, right? The vehicle skidded and they hopped out, he immediately scanned the ground for tire tracks. His heart sank. That's when he saw them, thick and deep in a patch of wet soil leading away into another area just off to the right. As they came around a large cluster of trees, a military Jeep was parked just out of view. Anxiety and fear took hold as they picked up the pace knowing that it would take another forty-five minutes if they walked. They pulled up their rifles, preparing for the unexpected.

They ran in silence. Chase's thighs screamed in protest but he pushed the pain from his mind. As they got nearer, they slowed their pace to a crawl when they came across the body of a soldier. Chase gave him a kick to make sure he was dead. Blood trickled from his mouth. There was an eerie silence to the camp. Only the sounds of birds could be heard, no shouting, crying or yelling.

Every few yards they would see another dead soldier. They had fought back. Survived? Moving quietly, they entered through the letterbox and came out into the clearing. Slumped down at the bottom of the large boulder was Harvey Crumlin. Chase rushed over to him and placed his hand on his neck, checking for a pulse. Nothing. He was gone. He made a gesture with two fingers for Daniel to check the first cabin. They cleared it, going room by room. Inside one of them, Chase turned his eyes away from the sight of Bridget. She'd been stabbed multiple times in the chest, and had her throat slit. A pool of blood had formed around her, her head slumped over.

As they came out, and searched the remainder of the camp, they found five more dead Koreans. They all looked as if they were pushing up towards the lookout tower but hadn't made it.

He wanted to yell out Matt's name but he didn't know how many soldiers there were, and if all of them were dead. As they got closer to the top of the incline that led to the wooden overlook, he scanned the area for more threats. No longer able to contain himself, he called out, "Matt!"

"Dad."

"Matt?" His heart leapt inside him at the sound of his son. At the top of the lookout, Matt appeared, looking down on them. Beside him were Alisa, Christine and Nancy, who was holding the baby. All four were armed, and looked terrified.

Chapter 13

"Get those kids away from here now!" Brody shouted to Todd.

Brody looked down the road as he guided the kids out of the truck and off towards the embankment. There was a curve on the road, and the only thing covering their asses was a huge cluster of trees that edged up against the side of the road. They knew they only had minutes before they would be overwhelmed by the enemy. They would have easily seen the smoke from the explosion several miles away. It swirled above them, a black inky mass staining the sky.

"Marlin, you got any more C4?"

"Yeah, why?"

"We need to make this look like a crash so they don't come looking for the kids." He took some of the C4 and planted it on the underside of the engine. Without the detonator, it wouldn't explode. With the kids safely out of sight, he hopped into the front of the truck and veered it towards the steep incline to make it look like they had tried to avoid the explosion and had crashed the truck. On the seat beside him was a portable military two-way radio. It was crackling away. Every few seconds he could hear Koreans speaking on it. Brody snatched it up and pocketed it. The truck barreled towards the ditch, and he jumped out at the last minute and it crashed into a tree. He scrambled to his feet and burst across the road to where the others were in the tree line while shouting for Marlin to light it up.

Another all mighty explosion and the entire thing was engulfed in flames. They didn't stick around to see who was coming but made their way deeper into the woods, away from the crash site.

Brody turned back once they reached a rise. Over the treetops he could see plumes of smoke swirling up towards the clouds, and drifting across the landscape. The sound of soldiers yelling could be heard. They pressed on, trying to lead the kids to safety.

The radio crackled on the side of his hip, and he yanked it off.

"Brody, come in," Chase said.

"Go ahead."

There was a pause. "Is Marlin nearby?"

Brody looked up as they trudged through the wilderness away from the town. His mind was still preoccupied by the whereabouts of his daughter. "No, what's up?"

"They're dead."

Brody slowed his pace coming to almost a complete stop. Dolman noticed his expression change.

"Bridget, Amanda, Harvey and Todd's mother."

"And Matt and the baby?"

"They're alive, so are Nancy, Alisa and Christine."

He contemplated what it meant before replying. "Copy that."

Static came over the speaker as the bad news sank in. He cast a glance up towards Marlin who was oblivious to it all. His eyes darted over to Todd. They were going to

211

be heartbroken, utterly destroyed.

"What is it, Brody?" Dolman asked making his way to the back of the line. It was pointless keeping it from him. He quietly shared the news, Dolman exhaled hard while running a hand over his smoke-covered face. On one hand, he wanted to tell Marlin and Todd right then but there was no telling how they would react. As it was they had enough on their hands with the group of kids. Most of them were between the ages of ten and fifteen.

"And Brody, one of Cyrus's men was among the dead. He led them up here. Those bastards did this."

It was clear they had been used like a pawn in a game of chess. Cyrus had gained their trust and at the first sign of trouble had turned on them. Why? That was still to be known. But something was clear, the first chance Brody got, he was going to kill him.

Brody brought the radio back up to his mouth. "Chase, you remember that secondary site that we found near Deer Mountain? You think you can make it to there?"

"Yeah. I'll gather up what we can carry from here and head out."

"I'll have one of us bring the kids up to there."

Deer Mountain was not far from Dry Creek Road. Five weeks ago, they had been scouting out new locations in the event that an emergency arose and they needed to move. There was an incredible spot on Deer Mountain that was hidden away in the forest. There were no trails or roads that led up to it. They had simply come across it after hiking through the outback. It was a secluded spot that was hard to reach even by foot but its proximity to a lake provided the same if not better protection and resources than what Iron Mountain had. Nestled in the pine forest, they had tossed around the idea of moving there because it was closer to the town of Mammoth. Chase had said that it almost looked as if someone had leveled out the forest in that area, in an attempt to build on it. At a glance it looked to be about thirty-seven acres of land. A pocket of paradise, were the words Chase used.

"Did you get Ava?"

"No."

"I'm sorry, man."

"We'll find her. She has to be on one of the other trucks."

Brody tried to remain positive, but he would have been lying to say that he wasn't worried. His mind was still in shock. After getting off the radio, he turned to Dolman.

"What am I going to say?"

"Tell them the truth. They deserve to hear it."

"Do you want to do it?"

"No, I think it should come from you."

"But you're trained in giving people bad news."

He scoffed. "Brody, the amount of training they gave us on delivering news to a deceased's loved one amounts to about ten seconds. No one can be prepared for that. All you can do is let them know you can't imagine what it's like and ask if there is anyone you can call to come and sit with them. That's it. You remain at their home until a family member arrives or until you hear otherwise. It's not easy."

"Who should we send up with the kids?"

"I think we should all go. Bury the dead and then figure out the next plan of attack."

"And leave my kid down there? No way," Brody said.

Dolman became the voice of reason that he needed to hear at that time. Had it just been him, he would have charged off allowing his emotions to cloud his judgment.

"Brody. There's not much that can be done right now," Dolman said. "We have just tossed a stone in the hornet's nest. They are going to have that place locked down. We know where they're going, so let's give the others time to bury the dead and grieve."

Reality was he didn't want to face them.

Brody looked ahead at Marlin who was chatting away to Todd. It wasn't that he had to tell them that their loved ones were dead. It was the fact that he knew Marlin would blame him. But it wasn't his fault. He hadn't led them up the mountain. The two men from Cyrus's group had been scouting in the area looking for them based on information given by those who remained in Crestwood Hills. He cast a glance over to Donahue. He'd been very vocal to the neighbors about their bunker. Could he have told someone? He shook his head. It didn't matter. There was no point stirring up even more animosity among the group. They needed each other now if they were ever to stand a chance against the troops and get Ava back.

They trudged on for what felt like hours before they reached Deer Mountain. There was a sense of accomplishment and yet at the same time they all knew that they had barely scratched the surface.

Chase and Matt met them at the edge of the second camp. They'd already pitched tents and started a small fire. Daniel was collecting water from a nearby stream when they arrived. There was a lot of hugging and pats on the back initially and then Marlin with a grin on his face began looking over the tops of everyone's faces.

"Amanda?"

Chase looked at Brody. "You didn't tell him?"

"I…" Brody gulped. "I thought it best we wait until we were far enough away from the troops. You know, with…"

Marlin pushed through a group of kids. "Where is she, Chase? Where's Amanda?"

Todd also was beginning to look concerned.

"They um…"

Before Chase could say it, Brody said it for him. "She's dead, Marlin."

His face went a ghostly white as the blood ran out of it. He staggered back a little.

"And my mother?" Todd asked.

Neither of them had to say anything, he knew. Todd dropped down to a crouch and placed both hands over his face. The expression on Marlin's face was like watching a pressure cooker.

"Where is she?" Todd asked.

"We couldn't bring her. They are back at the other camp."

He rocked back and forth and Chase placed a hand

on his shoulder. "I'm sorry, man." A few tears streaked his cheeks and he wiped them away. He got up, kicked a chair and walked off.

"Todd," Brody said.

He didn't respond and they knew it was best to give him some room. Marlin on the other hand was completely beside himself. He was pacing back and forth, with a clenched fist to his lips. Breathing heavily and looking as if he was about to explode. No one wanted to say a word to him but Dolman tried.

"Marlin."

He brought up a finger. "Stay away from me."

He slapped a palm into his chest and bolted into the surrounding forest, heading in the direction of Iron Mountain. For a few seconds they stood there unsure of what to say or do. They had the kids to think about now and even more responsibility on their plate.

"We should go, follow him. Just to make sure he doesn't do anything stupid."

"I think we are beyond people doing stupid things,"

Brody said. "I'll go."

Dolman stepped in. "No. You are the last person he is going to want to see."

"It wasn't his fault," Chase said.

"I'm not saying it was but after the disagreements they've had, Marlin is going to be looking for someone to blame." He shifted his weight from one foot to the next and placed a hand on his sidearm before scratching his head.

"Someone has to go. You know he won't just return. He'll probably head down to Mammoth and get himself killed."

Brody ran a hand over his chin. "We can't stay here for long anyway. They will be sending troops out to search for us. That crash might have bought us a little time but once they see there are no dead bodies inside they are going to know, if they don't already. They will hunt us down."

"Let them," Todd said walking back over. "I'm tired of hiding in the shadows." It was clear they had to do something but what? The soldiers would be more vigilant the next time around and they needed to get into Bishop.

"What if we do the exact opposite and turn ourselves in?"

"Are you crazy?" Chase said to Kai.

Kai came walking over, cradling his AR-15 and glancing around every so often. It was nerves. All of them were on edge. There was no telling if they had been followed or if troops had been sent out.

"I don't mean all of us. Just a few."

"This isn't the time for games, Kai," Dolman said.

"No, let him speak," Brody said, curious about what he had in mind.

"Okay, I'm more than a little disturbed by your idea, but go ahead, I'm all ears," Chase said leaning back against a tree.

"They sent up several men to kill us or take us in. What if I go back with one or two of you, dressed in one of the Korean uniforms?" He smirked. "I mean let's face it. Marlin was always going on about how we all look the same. Chinese, Koreans. There really isn't much difference. I actually can speak some Korean."

"Trojan horse style. I like it, even if it is mad," Chase said nodding. "But there's only one problem. What happens if they don't recognize you as one of the ones that were sent up? What happens if…"

"You're not looking at the big picture here, Chase. All we need to do is get on the inside. The rest of you can create a distraction while we try to arm some of the prisoners. You'll take out the checkpoint outside of Bishop and create enough noise and chaos to draw their attention away."

"Yeah, but what if it doesn't work?" Dolman asked.

"It has to," Brody spoke up. "I'm with you. I'll go with you."

Chase blew his cheeks out and tapped his foot against the tree trunk.

"What?"

Chase shrugged. "Nothing."

"No, say your piece."

"It's reckless. Insane. And liable to get us all killed." He breathed in deeply. "But whenever has anything that we've done been anything less? I'm in."

Brody gave a faint smile.

"We still have C4, yeah?" Kai asked.

"That's Marlin's department. We'd need to go speak with him."

Kai shrugged. "Well then let's go."

* * *

Marlin slumped over the body of Amanda. He scooped up her head and the top half of her body and held her close to him. She'd been shot multiple times, one of which had opened up her neck. He rocked back and forth, as tears fell to the ground and mixed with blood.

He cast his eyes around the camp at the bodies of the enemy, and rage swelled up in his chest. His throat was burning and his heart pounding from having run non-stop. The cabins had been peppered by rounds, and blood trickled from the dead creating a mini stream in the earth.

"I'm sorry. I'm so sorry," he kept repeating over and over with his eyes closed. It felt like his heart had been torn out. She'd kept him sane through it all. Amanda was like his anchor through the most turbulent times in his life. The one person he could turn to and find solace. She understood him better than he did himself. Knew when to call him out on his bullshit and wasn't afraid to tell him when he was being an ass.

Now she was gone.

Nothing good remained.

His jaw clenched together and his grip on her tightened. In that moment he felt more alone than he ever had. Only the sound of the wind could be heard whistling through the trees. The cold nipped at his ears, chilling him to the bone. How long he remained there was unknown to him, all he knew was that when he heard boots approaching he didn't move. If it was more troops he was ready to die with her. He knelt there clutching her tightly when he felt a hand touch him on the back.

"Marlin."

It took a second or two before he snapped out of the dazed state. Marlin turned and glanced up at Brody. Coming into view beside him were Chase, Kai and Todd. He stared at them blankly unsure of what to say, his mind numb from shock. His eyes dropped away and returned to staring at Amanda. For the first time in his life he was ready to die for his country, not because of his own loss, but because he knew that he was just one of many that would lose their lives if they did nothing.

"We'll help you bury her," Chase said.

"I…"

"You want vengeance. So do we," Brody said. "And we aim to get it."

Chapter 14

Cyrus was thrown to the floor in front of Colonel Pak Chun. His knees scraped against the metal-grated floor. Blood dripped from his lip, and his vision was slightly blurred from the beating he'd just received. This was not how he'd envisioned it playing out. After witnessing how many troops there were, he knew they needed more people if they were going to save his family. Once Gus was killed, he figured Brody would go back on his word to help, and any chance of getting the others was shot.

So, initially he was going to take Ava and arrange to have her captured in order to force the others to help, but then Damon said that maybe an exchange would be more effective. If it came to light that they had information on the ones responsible for the attack on the soldiers the other night, perhaps it would give them leverage in negotiating for the release of his family. It was a ballsy move and for a short while it looked as if it was going to work.

That was until a truck full of kids went missing.

"Do I look like a fool?" Col. Chun asked, encircling him like a lion.

When Cyrus didn't answer, a soldier stepped forward and cracked him hard on the back of the legs forcing him onto his face. Cyrus began pleading and cowering. "I swear I don't know where they went."

"You expect me to believe that you weren't in some way behind their escape?"

"I'm telling you the truth. What would I have to gain by releasing them?"

"Freedom. Martyrdom."

All he could do was shake his head. Was this man insane? Did he think he was like some kind of kamikaze suicide pilot that was willing to take the fall for his country? He wasn't one to grovel at the feet of anyone but he knew that they wouldn't think twice about putting a bullet in his head. "It was probably them."

"Probably? But you said they were at this camp in the mountains," he bellowed, his accent thick, his English muddied.

"They are. I mean, they were there when we left. Contact your men. Find out."

He stopped in front of Cyrus and crouched down, taking a leather rod in his hand and putting a hand on either end. He placed it under his chin to bring his face up. "We have tried to make contact and they aren't answering. If you have led my men into a trap, I will execute you and your friends."

Cyrus shook his head, his mind churning over. "I'm telling you, I don't know what happened to those kids. We were not involved."

"Not even as a distraction?"

Cyrus looked him square in the eyes and shook his head. Now he could see why he thought he was behind it. He hadn't thought this through clearly. *Damon!* He gritted his teeth. Stupid idea to try and negotiate, it had only placed them in the bull's-eye. Now any attack on their military would be made to look like they were involved in some way. He racked his brain trying to think of a way out of it. Some way to get on his good side and prove his loyalty.

"Tell me. Do you wish to live?"

Cyrus nodded. "I do. Listen…" His mind had gone into overdrive now. He was reaching for anything to hold on to. It felt as if the colonel had him by the balls over a ravine and was threatening to drop him.

"The girl. The young girl we brought with us. She's the daughter of the one in charge. If you bring her out, they will surrender."

It wasn't what he had intended but these were desperate times and he wasn't going to die for anyone. American or not. It would mean nothing if he was lying on the ground with a bullet in his head.

The colonel leaned back against a desk and regarded him with a degree of skepticism.

"A girl. What is her name?"

"Ava."

"If that's so, why did you have her with you?"

His lips quivered as he ran through different reasons before deciding on one. "We brought her here as a demonstration to show that we were serious about helping."

"Helping?"

Why was he repeating everything he said? "Collaborating." Cyrus couldn't even read if he was buying it. His eyes drifted to the firearm at the colonel's waist.

"A little late now, she has been taken to Bishop along with the others."

"No, just listen. She's the ticket."

The colonel shook his head. "More lies. Take him away."

"No. No!" Cyrus yelled as two guards stepped forward and took him by the arms and dragged him out of the building he was in. He and the others were thrown into a truck to be taken to Bishop.

* * *

Silence permeated the camp on that quiet mountain. Brody stared out across the valley of rugged terrain. Smoke rose above the tree line in the distance, blotting out parts of the jagged mountains. The place they had come to call home was now more dangerous than ever. He would have taken a thousand days inside a bunker hiding away from black rain than facing this. At least there they were protected, together and unharmed.

After they buried the dead, Marlin remained there for a little longer at the foot of Amanda's grave. They had to leave soon before more troops arrived but Kai told Brody to give him ten minutes. In the meantime, they went through the camp searching for a Korean soldier whose height was similar to Kai's. It wasn't hard. There were several he could have chosen. Kai stripped one of his uniform and boots before disposing of the body. The rest they left where they were. They wanted to give the impression that despite the others dying on that mountain, one of them had managed to escape with a prisoner. It was decided Brody would be that prisoner;

the others would be involved in creating havoc at the Bishop checkpoints.

While the others gathered up what firearms and ammo they could, Brody went into the small hut that Dolman had built and switched on the radio. There was too much equipment to lug out so they would have to leave it behind for now. Brody turned the dial and scanned through multiple frequencies one last time, hoping to hear something, anything that might boost their morale but there was nothing but dead air. Not even the freedom broadcast was playing. He switched it off and sighed before pulling out a cigarette and lighting it.

"Brody, it's time to go," Chase said poking his head inside.

"Marlin ready?"

He gave a nod. "Yeah, he's not in a good state but at least he's not flying off the handle. I guess that's something to be thankful for."

Brody rose from his seat and looked around him. He had a feeling they wouldn't be seeing this place again.

It had served them well but like everything since the war had started, it was temporary. He shook his head. So many lives had been lost. They stepped outside and the others looked their way. Mack's words came to him, like a silent reminder beneath the chatter of his mind. Instead of allowing them to roll around in his head he said them out loud. "You will learn to perform at your best under the worst conditions because that is what the military will demand of you, that's what America expects of you. Get comfortable with discomfort."

None them responded as they were all familiar with it. Mack had repeated it countless times over the course of training them. He said there was a point that many a man got to in any area of life. A line in the sand, so to speak, at which a person would decide whether to push on against insurmountable odds or buckle. It was passed on to them to serve as a reminder, and if they ever needed to be reminded, it was now. They were no longer just five friends trying to survive an attack on America but brothers in arms, working towards freedom, for themselves, for their town and for their country.

* * *

When they returned to the second camp at Deer Mountain, they were surprised to find the group seated around a fire chatting. They had built a Dakota fire pit. It was a common type of fire used in Afghanistan. They were designed to avoid detection by the enemy. Flames were hidden below ground level. The pit itself was created a foot inside the earth so that the fire burned hotter and less smoke was produced. They all turned as they entered the camp and as they did the group divided and they saw two U.S. military guys. They didn't look as if they were injured. Donahue jumped to his feet and came over.

"They showed up an hour after you left."

"Who are they?"

"Marines."

"Well I know that, who are they, how did they end up here?"

Brody was curious but nervous at the same time. After Cyrus's betrayal, he'd wondered how many others might have jumped ship to save their own skin. Military uniforms meant nothing. They could be picked up in any military surplus store in America. The two men must have noticed their look of concern. One of them stood to his feet and made his way through the crowd of kids.

"I'm Private Griffin," he thumbed over his shoulder, "and that's Private Vaughn."

He began asking them what platoon they were from, what part of the United States they came from and a list of more questions that some might not have even bothered to ask but he wanted to make sure they weren't collaborators with the Russians. He'd heard of Russian spies back in the cold war. Okay, maybe he was overreacting but after the shit they had just been through, trust was at an all-time low.

"How did you find us?"

"Um. That's a bit of a long story. Our platoon came under attack prior to the arrival of the Russians and Koreans in Bishop. We were the only two to make it out alive. We've been waiting for another platoon who are heading down from the north."

"There's more of you?"

"Yeah, well, at least another seventeen marines. There were more but…" he trailed off and Brody could tell he was finding it difficult to deal with the loss of those in his team. "Anyway, we heard the explosion and saw smoke rising nearby and thought it was perhaps our boys. We arrived in time to see you ditch that truck and make a break for it. So we followed you. Figured you might be part of a larger resistance."

"We ain't no resistance."

"Sure as hell looked like that to me," Vaughn muttered coming into view and staring at all the kids. Vaughn was your typical clean-cut American, athletic, hair shaved short, and a jaw that looked as if it could take a punch. Griffin had an imposing stature, a full beard and arms that looked as if they had been stitched into his uniform. "You did one hell of a job taking down those soldiers."

Brody raised a finger for a moment and motioned

to Dolman. He walked a short distance away to make sure he was out of earshot.

"You trust these two?"

"Yeah, these seem legit."

"What, because of the uniforms?"

He cracked a smile. "No, Brody. Since they have been here they have been in radio contact with the platoon that's heading south right now."

"Did you speak to them?"

"No. But listened while he was in communication."

Brody nodded while eyeing them over his shoulder. They looked to be in good spirits. Vaughn went over to his backpack and pulled out a bag of hard candies and handed them out. On the surface, it all looked good but he was feeling jaded after all they'd been through.

"Anyway, did you get a uniform?"

"Yeah. Actually several."

"Several?"

"Figured you are going to need something to get close to that checkpoint."

Dolman looked over at Marlin. "How's he holding up?"

"Surprisingly well for someone who's just lost his entire world."

He frowned. "Yeah, that's got to hurt."

"You told them what we have planned?"

"Not yet."

"If you don't mind. Don't mention it to them at least until..."

"Right, you don't trust them."

"I didn't say that."

"But your face gives it away."

"That obvious?"

Dolman put his arm around his shoulder. "Come on, let's get some food going. If we are going to do this, we need to hit them at night. It gives us the best chance of creating confusion."

Each of them had brought a few cases of MRE's from the camp. It wasn't the best-tasting food but it would do the job. As they sat huddled around the fire at the beginning of the evening, Donahue, Kai, Todd and Rodriguez paced around the perimeter to keep an eye out for the enemy. Though they felt reasonably safe there, and no one else knew about the place, they weren't taking any chances.

Brody continued to grill the Marines on their lives before the military and what they knew about the situation as it unfolded during the past few months. No matter what questions he threw at them in an attempt to catch them off guard, they just came back with answers. Slowly but surely he began to believe they were the real deal. Government hadn't completely collapsed. The U.S. was fighting back and this was the first sign that America might rise from the ashes. It gave all of them hope, if only for a few hours.

Chapter 15

"Tell them to hold off on that plan, we are going to be delayed," Sergeant Westbury yelled into the radio while keeping his head down behind one of their trucks. After leaving Bridgeport, they had made it as far as Lee Vining before they had encountered another group of Russian soldiers. Upon arrival, the entire width of Highway 395 before them had been blocked off by multiple vehicles that someone had shifted into place. At first there was no sign of the enemy until they got closer and then rounds ricocheted off the sides of their armored truck, making it sound like the truck was being pelted by huge hailstones.

They had managed to back up and reverse into Murphey's Lodging, a quaint little chalet-style motel off the strip. Now outside of the vehicle, his team had spread out and was returning fire. Westbury was trying to get an idea of how many there were. After their last fight back in

Walker, it had taken them the better part of three hours to cut through a troop of eighteen Russians. They were tricky bastards to pin down.

"Sarge, I'm gonna take five guys across to Mono Lake Avenue and circle around onto Second Street. See if we can't hedge them in."

He gave a nod and darted out with three of his men towards Mono Coffee Cup, where several Russians were. As they made it to the corner of the lodging, they came under heavy fire from across the road.

"Bastards are like ants."

"We'll cut through the lodging, and out the back," Westbury said leading the men to the main entrance. From the moment he stepped inside, he could tell that something terrible had occurred there. There was blood splatter on the walls and the smell of death lingered in the air. Martinez pulled up a bandanna over the bottom half of his face. "This shit is nasty."

As they passed by the front desk in the lobby, they could see where the smell was coming from. Behind the counter were three civilians piled on top of each other, their limbs twisted up, their faces battered. They hadn't simply been shot, they had been tortured. He winced turning his eyes away and continued back through a set of doors into a darkened corridor. They pressed on towards the back portion of the motel, searching for an exit door. They found it smashed to pieces with a man laying prone on the ground. He still had a weapon in his hand, a huge meat cleaver. Another American attempting to fight back but he had taken a bullet to the head.

They stepped over him and were just about to exit when a bullet struck Westbury in the chest and he stumbled back into the arms of Martinez who dragged him inside while the other two returned fire.

The pain was intense but within a matter of seconds it began to ease. It had just hit his body armor.

"That was close, Sarge. You okay?"

"Yeah, just give me a minute."

He lay on the carpet caked in dry blood. The non-stop fighting since leaving Carson City was wearing them down. Even though they'd managed to get a good night's sleep in Bridgeport, the constant stress was tough. As he lay there on the floor trying to catch his breath, he remembered his time in Afghanistan. The number of good men that he'd held as they took their last breaths. The look of fear in their eyes. The final words — usually for family. War was nasty. There were no two ways about it. It changed men. Robbed them of their innocence and turned many into animals. He'd seen many a good man go through boot camp, eager to serve his country, only to be found months later cowering as mortars flew overhead. Every man was different in the heat of battle. Most rose to the occasion, almost fueled by the constant barrage of rounds being fired at them, but others shrank back, their face a picture of what was going through their mind. *Why did I sign up for this? I didn't think it was going to be like this. That damn military commercial left out this part.* Westbury shook off the pain and scrambled to his feet.

"Pull back, we'll find another way out."

They retreated into the darkness of the corridor.

His radio crackled.

"Sarge, come in," Parker said coming in over the speaker.

"Go ahead, Parker."

"We're gaining ground, but there is a shitload of them farther up. Should we engage?"

Martinez looked at him. Both of them look baffled by the question. It was in moments like this that he wanted to be sarcastic but instead he chose to tell him to hold off until they made it over to them.

"Martinez, Castillo, Rocco, check out the rooms, see if you can find a safe way to the other side."

They darted into individual rooms and one by one they moved up and down the hall trying to find one room that would give them access to the back of the café without being seen. He figured if they could get in the back, they could swing around on them. From what he was able to tell, there were four Russians positioned around the outside of the café. Two at the corners, another on the roof, and a fourth inside in one of the upper windows.

"Sarge!"

He bolted out of the room he was in and went four doors down and entered to find Castillo sliding back one of the windows. "The tree and bushes are blocking the view."

"Right, let's go."

One by one they crawled through the opening and dropped down to the backyard of the café. It was a two-story building, so there was a quite a drop. Once down they wouldn't be able to get back up again if things went south. Westbury was to be the last one out. He had just got one leg out of the window when he heard a sound behind him. It was sudden, like boots rushing towards the room. He wasn't going to give away their position so he slumped back inside and rolled behind the bed. A breeze moved the drapes in front of the window every so slightly. With one finger hovering over the trigger, his adrenaline kicked in. His heart pounded against his chest at the sound of Russian voices. Turning his head slightly to the right, he could see beneath the bed two sets of boots. One of them stepped inside. In an instant, he bolted upright and unleashed a flurry of rounds at the startled Russian soldier. The soldier flew backwards into his comrade, who took the full brunt of the rest of the shots. They didn't stand a chance. Westbury followed through by peppering the wall either side with multiple rounds to make sure if there were any others out in the corridor, they would be taken care of too. Moving fast, and keeping his rifle aimed at the door, he climbed out the window and dropped down, landing in a large bush. Even though it broke his fall, it still took the wind out of him.

"You just couldn't resist, could you, Sarge," Martinez said with a grin on his face before helping him up. They fanned out in combat intervals heading towards the rear of the café. The Russian had shifted his attention to Parker's team who were now heading down Second Street. They used that distraction to their advantage. As soon as they were inside, Martinez and Parker went to the front door while Westbury double-timed it up the stairs heading for the one on the second floor.

He heard gunfire down below before he burst into the room that was occupied by a sniper. As he came through the door he saw the rifle against the windowsill but no soldier. Before he had a chance to scan the room, a large mass came at him from behind the door. The Russian grabbed his rifle and forced him up against the wall and pushed it under his chin. The look of absolute hatred in his eyes only fueled Westbury to push back harder. He slammed a knee into his gut causing the Russian to ease off the pressure. But it wasn't enough. He wouldn't let go of the damn rifle. They plowed back and forth across the room, throwing each other into furniture. A mirror smashed and glass embedded into the Russian's back causing him to cry out in agony.

Instead of pushing away, Westbury pulled him in while at the same time head-butting him. The guy's nose exploded like a fire hydrant. And still he didn't release his grip. These Russians were suckers for punishment. The fight carried out into the corridor and this time the

Russian managed to bring him down to the floor. He landed hard and now had the guy's two hundred and twenty pounds weighing down on his chest. He was muttering something in Russian. Westbury knew if he didn't act fast he was going to run out of steam and find himself strangled to death by his own weapon. He pushed back as hard as he could, bench pressing him. Westbury brought his knees up and used them to springboard him off. As he did, the gun flew out of his hands and over the banister. The Russian collapsed against the drywall. Not wasting another second, he yanked free his KA-BAR knife and rushed him while he was still dazed. He stabbed him over and over again in the gut while holding a hand over his mouth to muffle his screams before slicing his neck from ear to ear.

Westbury staggered back, out of breath and energy. He slid the knife back into its sheath and reached for his Beretta M9 before scanning the second floor for any other potential threats. With the Russian out of the way, he went and retrieved his M16. After he climbed up to the next floor and found the fire escape which had been used by the soldier on top of the roof. Exhausted and in no state to deal with another fight, he yanked off a grenade, kept his thumb over the spoon as he pulled the pin, and then tossed it up onto the roof. He dived on to the floor near one of the beds. He heard the soldier curse and try to scramble before it went off. After that there was silence.

Westbury made his way down to the ground and came out to find Martinez smoking a cigarette.

"Are you kidding me?"

"What? The threat has been neutralized."

He got back on the radio. "Parker. Give me an update."

"We're still looking at least another ten, they've moved back to Third Street."

With that said, Westbury turned, snatched the cigarette out of Martinez's mouth and tossed it down. "We aren't done yet."

"Shit, Sarge, those are hard to come by now."

"So is human life. Move out!"

* * *

"They aren't going to be here for at least another hour, possibly two if they get held up any further."

"We don't have that kind of time," Donahue replied.

Brody looked up from the rough outline of Bishop that he was carving into the dirt with a large stick. He was in the middle of briefing everyone on the plan to enter and take out the men standing guard at the checkpoints.

"There are four major arteries into Bishop. Each one intersects with the city limits at the four corners. They are going to have each of those blocked off by checkpoints. We have Highway 395 to the northwest. That routes its way through the town, curving around to the south, which is where there will be another checkpoint. There is Highway 6 to the northeast corner and Highway 168 to the southwest. Now we really only have to concern ourselves with 395 and 168, but to do both checkpoints it's going to require more manpower, firepower and well, being as the Marines aren't going to

249

be arriving for a while, I'm thinking it's best we just focus on these two at the west side." He took a breath while looking over to Kai. "Now Kai is going to take me in with him, if everything goes well, we will enter with a truck via the northwest. Once inside, the aim is to get that truck as close as we can to the main center of operations. If we take out the head, chances are the rest are going to scatter. Now they are going to be expecting their men back soon, that's why we can't wait on this," he said turning towards the two Marines. "Time is of the essence here."

"Honestly, do you really think they are going to buy this?" Vaughn said. "This is not the right way to go about it. You have a better chance of getting your daughter back by waiting for the platoon to show up."

Marlin stepped forward. "This isn't just about his daughter." He cast a glance at Brody. "No offense, Brody."

"None taken."

"It's about every single person we have lost since this shit storm started. Family, friends, Americans. This is about taking back our home."

Griffin nodded. "I understand but you are not trained for this."

Marlin scoffed. "What, because we didn't go through twelve weeks of being shafted at Uncle Sam's boot camp? Buddy," he motioned with his thumb to those around him. "That boot camp you went through was like child's play compared to what Mack put us through."

Vaughn screwed up his face. "Who the fuck is Mack?"

"Hey, show some fucking respect!" Todd said while jabbing his finger in his face.

Brody tried to be a voice of reason in it all as he could clearly see they were confused. As much as he appreciated what Marlin was saying, what Mack had put them through couldn't be compared to real Marine Corps training.

"What my friends here are trying to say, is we appreciate your advice but those people down there need our help and right now the window of opportunity is getting smaller by the minute. We have to do this now. We can't wait around for the others."

Vaughn shook his head. "Then it's your funeral."

"Whatever, pal," Marlin said. "Thank God I didn't join the Marines."

Griffin didn't say anything. He looked down at the map of Bishop etched into the ground and exhaled hard as if he was coming to terms with the fact that they were going whether the Marines were with them or not.

"Brody, take us through what you had in mind."

Vaughn looked back at him with a look of confusion, perhaps disgust. In all honesty there was a high probability that it wouldn't work but they had to take that chance. There was no way in hell he was going to leave Ava down there among those animals.

Chapter 16

The first thing on the agenda that night was obtaining the military Jeep the Koreans had originally driven to the end of Deadman Creek Road. Beneath the Jeep itself Marlin planted multiple sticks of C4, then handed a remote detonator to Kai. The first stage of the mission was to enter Bishop, locate the main center of operations and draw out the leader. Once he was within spitting distance Kai would detonate the C4 and God willing, he and a whole whack of those Korean bastards were going up in a cloud of smoke.

Though, to ensure that all went off without a hitch, Marlin would create a distraction at the northeast checkpoint while some of the others would veer off Highway 395, go south on Ed Powers Road and then hang a left and do the same at the checkpoint on Highway 168. It required meticulous timing, and if they were honest, a degree of luck. The idea was simple —

create so much confusion inside Bishop that the troops would be divided. If they could breach the two checkpoints, free some of the people of Bishop, they had a fighting chance. It would be bloody, and lives would be lost. There was no way to cherry coat it, or even lessen the blow.

It seemed as if their whole lives had been gearing up for this one event.

All of them were to rendezvous several miles north of Highway 203. It was a quiet journey out to meet them. For the first twenty minutes, no words were exchanged between them. The weight of what lay ahead bore down.

"You know there is a good chance we won't make it out," Kai said as he stared ahead at the road that was lit up by his high beams. He adjusted his grip on the wheel and swallowed hard.

"Yeah, I know," Brody replied.

"Man, life has not worked out the way I thought it would." Kai sniffed hard. "I always wondered what it would be like if we had all made it into the military and were sent off to war." He let out a nervous chuckle. "You know, back when we were just kids it all seemed…"

"Like a commercial?" Brody asked finishing what he was saying.

He snorted. "Yeah."

"Well that's what the military is good at. Selling the dream. So does every profession."

"Yeah, I mean, I don't know about you but I always had these grandiose ideas of heading off to boot camp, getting shouted at, graduating in front of my parents and feeling this pride welling up inside me, then getting shipped out to some foreign shithole. Parachuting in like heroes, fucking up a few power-hungry assholes and returning to the USA to the sound of cheers. But it's not like that, is it?"

"Never is. But hey, at least this way we get to stare the enemy in the face before it's lights out."

There was silence as they drove back through the winding roads with tall pine trees flanking them on either side. The silhouette of jagged mountaintops rose in the distance. That evening a crescent moon was riding high in the sky, lighting up the night.

"You think he would have been proud?"

"Your father?"

"No. Mack."

Brody laughed. "I think he would tear us a new one with the way we have acted since this has kicked off." Brody stared up into the night sky. "But yeah, I would like to think he's looking down on us, watching our backs and cheering us on."

"Go get those fuckers!" they both said, almost in unison before letting out a laugh.

"I miss him," Kai said.

"Yeah, me too."

Mack had always spoken about fate, and their lives being nothing more than fallen leaves on the surface of a stream, flowing down towards some final obscure destination. He didn't understand it then but now he did. Much of what he had shared with them made sense now. Mack wasn't just some old coot reliving his military years through a bunch of troubled kids, he truly was preparing the next generation for what he feared would happen to the nation.

When they finally arrived at the turnoff for 395, Marlin and the others were already there, waiting. There were two large military trucks that they had obtained from somewhere, with enough room in the back to fill with at least ten people. Kai veered off to the hard shoulder and hopped out. It was the final time they would be all together before Bishop.

"Where did you manage to dig these up?" Brody asked.

"Seems our Marine boys here are more resourceful than I gave them credit," Marlin said eyeing them both. Originally Vaughn was going to hang back and keep an eye on the kids but Alisa and Nancy and Dolman's wife opted to do it. They had proven themselves as a force to be reckoned with. Chase didn't want Matt coming along but he was old enough to hold a gun, and after the assault on Iron Mountain, and with the pure number of troops they were about to go up against, he soon let it slide. In many ways they had bonded and become even closer through the events that had transpired.

Vaughn was back on the communications channel speaking with the platoon.

"Well can you at least give me an ETA on when you might be here?" He paused. "Yeah, they are going in."

Brody could hear the voice of some sergeant on the other end telling him that it was unclear, as they had encountered a large unit of Russians who were keeping them from venturing south.

"So basically we are shit out of luck?"

"Private, hand the radio to whoever is in charge of this harebrained idea."

He held the radio up to his chest. "He wants a word with whoever is in charge. Is that you?" he said motioning to Brody.

"Me? No."

The others looked his way. "Dolman, why don't

you speak to him?"

"I don't see how it's going to be of much use but I'll take it."

He handed off the radio and Dolman walked a short distance away so he could converse. The rest of them looked agitated. They scanned the road for troops. There were twelve of them including the two Marines. When they ambushed the checkpoints, there would be five attacking from the northwest, and five from the southwest.

Todd gripped his stomach. "I think I'm gonna hurl."

He began retching and making these foul sounds.

Marlin backed up and pushed him towards the tree line. "Shit dude, well don't do it near my feet, go over there." Brody's own stomach was doing flips. Nerves were getting the better of them all. They were about to enter the lion's den and go to war.

Dolman raised his voice and sounded as if he was arguing with the sergeant. Eventually he made his way over and tossed the radio back to Vaughn.

"So?"

"We're going in."

Vaughn scowled. "You have to got to be kidding."

"You don't like it, stay here," Dolman snapped back. Brody understood Vaughn's hesitation. Under any other conditions they would have hung back and waited for the rest of the troops to arrive but these weren't ordinary conditions. Lives were at stake and by now they would be expecting the return of the unit that headed up to Iron Mountain.

"Well, are you ready to do this?"

Kai placed the Korean soldier's cap on his head.

"I told you he would pass for one," Marlin said. Todd had one hand against a tree and tossed up whatever he had for lunch before he wiped his mouth and returned.

"Now is everyone clear about what they are to do?" Dolman asked. Everyone nodded and got into the vehicles. The tension was thick as they prepared to roll out. Brody slapped on a pair of handcuffs but didn't fully engage them. M16s were in the rear of the vehicle and he had a Beretta stashed in the small of his back. Kai was kitted out in uniform and looking every bit the part as the Jeep rumbled out onto the highway and headed towards Bishop. It would take just under forty minutes to reach the checkpoint.

"What if they recognize you're not one of them?"

"They won't."

"But if they do?"

Kai turned and shot him a sideways glance. "Then, I guess this is the end of the road."

It wasn't exactly what he was hoping to hear, but what else could be said? The plan wasn't airtight. Any number of things could go wrong, from the Koreans not letting them through the checkpoint to someone recognizing that he wasn't part of their unit. The others would follow. Kai had told them to give it a good five to ten minutes so they could get into the heart of Bishop, then he would signal them using the radio.

As they got closer to the checkpoint, their

conversation ceased and Brody felt fear shoot through him. He had to keep reminding himself why he was doing this. He looked down at the photo of Ava in his hands before tucking it into his shirt pocket.

Bright lights were shone in their faces as the Jeep approached the checkpoint. There were four Koreans guarding the station. Two in a Jeep, and two standing behind a gated barricade made of steel, like the kind seen outside concerts to keep people from spilling out into the street.

. Kai eased off the gas as the two soldiers gestured where he had to stop. One of them had his rifle up and was pointing, while the other drifted his flashlight beam across their faces. Brody squinted and turned slightly. His pulse was racing as a soldier came up to the passenger side and looked in, while the other one spoke with Kai on the driver's side.

Kai had told him in advance that he would only say a few words, just enough for them to know who Brody was and that he was the only one who had survived from the unit that was sent up to bring back resistance members.

The soldier frowned and angled his light directly into Brody's face. He muttered a few more words and then yelled to the other two in the nearby Jeep. They hopped out and went about moving back the barricade before waving them through. It was definitely one of those moments where he wanted to pinch himself. It had worked!

"Goddamn," Brody muttered under his breath.

"Shhhh," Kai replied while keeping a stern look on his face.

The Jeep rumbled in and his eyes opened at the sight of what they had established in a short amount of time inside Bishop. A constant hum could be heard coming from generators that were powering large spotlights, like the kind seen at construction sites, except these weren't hoisted high up but positioned on top of the buildings, angled down in various areas. Not every area of the street was lit up but they had certainly done a good job of making sure that nothing escaped their eye.

Many of the side streets were blocked off with school buses and large military trucks, the kinds that carried ammo and weapons. Brody watched as they unloaded multiple metal cases.

"You think they dropped those from a plane?"

"That or they have taken them from our military."

It was tough to tell at a glance how many of them there were, just that it was more than they had seen in Mammoth. Residents were absent from the streets. Either they had rounded them up and carted them out of Bishop, or they had them in a secure location. Brody was thinking the Tri County Fairgrounds or Bishop City Park. It was a wide-open space that would be easy enough to secure with a perimeter of fencing.

A Korean soldier yelled and directed Kai to veer off and follow a street that led down to a building that housed the *Inyo Register*. It was a large red building on the curve of Highway 395 before it headed south.

"You better call it in," Brody said as more soldiers

gestured where they were to park. Kai picked up the radio, and gave the signal. Now their lives were in the hands of their friends.

Sure enough, straight across the road from what they believed to be the main center of operations was a large number of residents. The Tri County Fairgrounds was already fenced off. Though the fence wasn't high, it certainly worked as a great place to enclose the masses of people. Off to the left of that was a storage facility, and by the looks of it they were using that to hold even more prisoners.

A Korean soldier approached them and muttered something to Kai, he replied and got out and came around to get Brody. He manhandled him in a fashion that would lead them to believe he felt nothing for him. Brody couldn't help wonder if Kai was getting a kick out of it as a form of retribution for what he'd done prior to leaving the first camp. To make it look like he'd been in an assault on Iron Mountain, he struck Kai in the mouth, cutting his lip, and then had him slice a portion of his arm to make it bleed.

Now here he was getting kicked to the ground in front of several soldiers.

Brody couldn't understand a fucking word of what they were saying but he got the impression that whoever was in charge of them was busy, and he was being told to wait as Kai remained at his side, holding a Beretta to his head.

While they waited, Brody turned his head ever so slightly and looked back at the field full of people, a mix of Bishop and Mammoth residents that had been carted in by the truckload. Ava was among them somewhere. *Where are you?*

A sudden whack on the top of his head and he felt warm blood trickling down. A Korean soldier had stepped forward and was yelling at him. He hadn't a clue what the man was saying but he figured he must have known one or more of the troops that had been killed on Iron Mountain. He slapped Brody across the face and he tumbled over onto his side. He felt the Beretta stashed in the back of his jeans slipping. *Shit,* that was the last thing he wanted to fall out. *Not now. Not here.*

In that moment two things happened. First a large Korean soldier stepped out from the front entrance of the building yelling, then his eyes fell upon Brody. Fear shot through him. There was a very strong possibility he was about to die.

C'mon guys, where are you?

Chapter 17

Shrouded in darkness, the Korean uniform would be all they could see. Marlin kept his head low as the military truck approached the checkpoint. With one hand on the wheel and the other holding a Beretta pointed at the door, he was prepared for the worst. Beside him Daniel was armed and hunched over.

"How come I ended up with the smallest uniform?" he said, pulling at the top as Marlin eased off the gas, and the truck rolled up in front of the barrier. One of the Korean soldiers had his hand up and the other on his K1A.

"Keep it down," he muttered, glancing up with his eyes as the two soldiers divided and went either side of the truck. He saw two more in the Jeep watching carefully. The soldier banged on the side. In that moment, two things happened: the two Marines rolled out from underneath the truck and squeezed the triggers on their

M16s, while Todd slipped out from the back of the truck, pulled a pin and tossed a grenade at the Jeep. Everything occurred in a matter of seconds. Only one of the men in the Jeep reacted and dived out before the grenade went off, and Daniel took him down by leaning out of the window and firing three rounds in rapid succession. It was over in under a minute.

The Marines rushed forward and scooped up the fallen soldiers' weapons and ammo before moving the barrier so they could squeeze through. Once in, they hopped back on board. No time was spent high-fiving, or saying job well done. They had only scraped the surface of what was about to turn into a brutal battle.

Marlin had Amanda's face at the forefront of his mind as he smashed the accelerator and they pressed on. This was it. Do or die.

* * *

At almost the same time on the southwest side of Bishop, the truck with Chase driving drew close to the checkpoint.

"Shit!" he muttered under his breath. Instead of four soldiers, there were seven. Another military truck had pulled up just as they arrived. They were probably changing the guards. Under the bright lights they could see them chatting among themselves as the truck rumbled towards them. Several of them looked their way and he just had this gut feeling it wasn't going to go well.

Chase slammed on the brakes sixty feet away from the checkpoint. He had to think fast. The truck had been rigged with C4 and was to be used as a weapon once they got inside but it looked like they were going to need it now. In the distance he could see two of the guards starting to take notice. Chase opened the door slightly and yelled down to Dolman and Rodriguez who were underneath.

"Change of plans. Get out the rear now and take Matt. Move it!"

He glanced back to see four soldiers slowly heading their way.

As they were so far back from the checkpoint, the

vehicle was still enveloped by the darkness of the night, providing the cover that was needed. All they would have been able to see were the two headlights cutting into the night. Either side of the road was nothing but open landscape. A small number of trees, and tons of sagebrush.

Chase turned to Donahue. "Get out."

"What are you going to do?"

"It's time to bounce. Now move it."

"No, if you're staying in, so am I."

"Suit yourself, but when I tell you to jump, you better jump!"

"What?"

Chase gunned the engine and the truck tore forward.

"Are you out of your mind?" Donahue yelled.

Chase let out a laugh. "Let's find out. Now keep your head down."

The wind howled through the open window, as the truck barreled forward. Chase gripped the detonator in one hand while keeping his eyes on the road ahead. The soldiers ahead reared up their rifles and unleashed a flurry of rounds.

"Get out now!" Chase yelled as he pushed open his door and jumped. His body slammed into the ground and he rolled. He saw Donahue on the other side of the road disappear into the ditch. The truck roared on while the soldiers continued to fire at it. As the soldiers scurried to get out of the way, the truck slammed into their barrier pushing it back several feet but bringing it to a grinding halt. The soldiers could be heard yelling and pointing their guns up at the truck's cabin, expecting someone to get out, but they'd already shifted ass. Chase brought up the detonator.

"This is for Bridget. Assholes!"

He pressed the button and the truck lifted off the ground several feet in a giant explosion that knocked the soldiers back. It took out five of the soldiers and left the other three temporarily blinded by the blast.

"Move in," Donahue yelled scrambling up the

ditch's incline and heading towards what remained of the checkpoint. The assault was fast and deadly. Both Donahue and Chase took out the remaining soldiers as they rolled around on the ground gripping their eyes in agony. Chunks of shrapnel were embedded in their skin. Killing them was the most humane thing they could have done. They would have eventually bled out anyway.

"We need to move fast, more will be coming."

They jumped into the truck the additional soldiers had arrived in and Chase fired up the engine. They took off towards West Line. The hope was that they would be able to get down one of the side streets before another unit headed their way.

"God, I hope Kai managed to come through on his end."

* * *

It was a sweet sound. The explosions echoed across the town of Bishop. A plume of smoke rose in the distance full of fire. Some of the soldiers that had been milling around the main center of operations cradled their rifles and took off on foot, while others jumped into trucks and Jeeps and tore out of there.

Kai grabbed a hold of Brody by the scruff of the neck and hauled him up to take him away to the containment area where they were holding residents. He'd only made it a few steps when a gruff voice barked at him to stop. Kai turned and faced the one he'd heard the soldiers calling Colonel Pak Chun. The stern-looking man approached asking him what had happened to his unit.

"It was a surprise attack, Colonel."

He eyed him with a look of suspicion, casting his eyes up and down him. Kai swallowed hard. He figured the gig was up and they were screwed, and for a second the colonel looked as if he was about to say something when one of his men came rushing over to tell him that they were under attack from the west side.

He barked out a few commands and Kai used the opportunity to walk away. He had no idea about protocol. Whether he was meant to salute him or remain standing where he was.

"Soldier."

Kai looked over his shoulder.

"Good job."

He nodded, then gave a salute before shuffling away. They had only made it a few feet across the road when he heard his voice again. This time Kai froze.

"Does this belong to you?"

With one hand on Brody, and the other in his pocket on the detonator, he considered for a second pushing the button but instead turned. The colonel approached them holding what looked like a photo. His eyes darted to Brody who appeared horrified. It was a photo of Ava. The colonel stared down at it as he stood before them.

"Is this your daughter?"

Brody nodded.

"You were part of the resistance that killed my men?"

To that he didn't respond. A bead of sweat formed

on Kai's brow. His eyes bounced between the colonel who was intently focused on Brody and two more soldiers who were standing nearby.

In an instant the colonel lashed out and knocked Brody to the ground. Brody went to get up and he was struck again before the colonel crouched down and tore up the photo in front of him and then dropped the small fragments all over his face.

"Take him away."

Kai moved in fast before he changed his mind. He'd had his hand close to his sidearm, ready to shoot if the colonel had gone for his weapon. Though what concerned him more were the two soldiers standing nearby. They were talking among themselves, and though he couldn't hear all they said, he picked up on some of it. It was more than enough. They were discussing the unit that had left for Iron Mountain. The largest of the two said he knew them, and that he didn't recall Kai being one of them. He threw out enough doubt to cause the two of them to begin making their way over. Kai was hoping for the colonel to head back before he pushed the trigger but as the two soldiers walked past the Jeep, he pressed the button.

The blast knocked them all back. Kai landed hard on the ground sending him unconscious. When he came to, there was ringing in his ears and his body ached. With his vision blurred and smoke drifting across the parking lot, it was hard to make out anything. All around him there was debris from the vehicle, plus chunks of stone and wood where it had torn apart the corner of the building. Several bodies of fallen soldiers lay nearby. He squinted hard, rubbed his head and the world around him snapped back into view. Amid the smoke he could see Brody with his arm wrapped around the neck of the colonel as he backed up from three soldiers who had their rifles leveled at him. All of them were yelling.

* * *

After the explosion, Brody thought Kai was dead. Acting quickly, he pulled his wrists out of the unlocked cuffs, retrieved the Beretta from his waistband and moved in on the colonel before soldiers swarmed them. Shaken, and barely comprehending what had taken place, the colonel didn't put up much resistance when Brody put him in a chokehold with one arm while holding the Beretta out at the approaching soldiers.

"Get back!"

He pressed the gun against the colonel's temple and shuffled towards the wall of the building. He figured if he could at least get inside, he might prevent an attack from behind him.

The three soldiers were yelling in Korean, no doubt telling him to put the gun down. He figured they weren't stupid enough to try and take a shot at him. The colonel yelled at them and because they didn't put down their weapons, he assumed they had been told to take the shot. Using him as a human shield, he continued to back up until he saw Kai stagger to his feet, withdraw his handgun and squeeze off a round at one of the soldiers. Brody did the same with another, and the two of them dropped. Kai took out the third with a single round.

The colonel must have known what was about to happen next. Brody turned the gun on him and pressed it into his temple. In one defiant act, the colonel shouted in broken English, "You'll never win. This country is—"

Brody squeezed off a round before he could finish and brain matter shot out the other side of his head as a red mist sprayed across Brody's face.

"Our home, asshole!"

Brody released the colonel's limp body, and it dropped to the ground.

It was a chaotic scene. The smoke from the now burnt-out Jeep had spread across the road providing much-needed concealment and yet at the same time they knew that more soldiers would be heading their way. Brody shoved the Beretta into the front of his waistband and scooped up a K2 assault rifle and some extra ammo, along with a couple of grenades. Kai did the same.

Running at a crouch they circled the building to try and find a vehicle. Kai tore off the cap and jacket he was wearing. Several soldiers rushed out the back of the building and were quickly gunned down by them. Every so often they could hear explosions coming from the west. From their vantage point they could see the residents in the Tri County Fairgrounds. Soldiers in charge of watching over them looked to be in a state of panic.

"Over here," Kai said pointing to a truck. They hurried over and hopped in. Kai started the engine and peeled out under a hail of gunfire.

"Where now?"

"Straight into the fairgrounds."

He didn't question his direction. Kai crushed the accelerator to the metal. Swerving erratically to avoid the onslaught of rounds being fired at them, the truck burst out of the lot causing them to bounce in their seats. The vehicle careened through a turn, and smashed straight through a chain-link fence. Brody leaned half of his body out of the passenger side window and squeezed off rounds, taking down startled soldiers. Soldiers fanned out after he yanked a grenade and tossed it overhead causing an epic eruption as it ignited a propane tanker. Several of the residents turned on nearby soldiers and began to fight back. Many were gunned down, but it was hard to control hundreds of determined residents. It was a beautifully chaotic scene. Fueled by adrenaline, panic and the will to survive, Mammoth and Bishop residents worked together to bring down soldiers. After a few had been taken out, and guns had made their way into the hands of Americans, there was a sense that they were gaining ground. Now it wasn't just their small group fighting for freedom, it was all of them. They were nothing but the spark to ignite the fuel.

He looked off across the field as another truck barreled through on its way to the west. There was no telling how well the others were doing but if the smoke and fire coming from the distance was any sign of the damage the others were inflicting, then all was good.

Brody tapped Kai on the shoulder and told him to ease off the gas as he was going in circles so he could get clear shots off at the soldiers around the perimeter. Now he needed to find Ava. Brody jumped out of the truck and grabbed up a jacket that was on the ground and tossed it back into the truck.

"You might want to put this on, otherwise you are going to get shot."

That was the downside to having entered the town with the intent to convince them that he was a Korean soldier. Now that residents were fighting back, he was liable to end up with a bullet in him if he didn't change out of that uniform.

Brody continued to fire at soldiers who were now pulling back while Kai hopped out of the truck.

He shouted to those who had taken back weapons from the Koreans.

"Jump in," he shouted to residents who were armed. "Help the others on the west side." He watched as eight men and two women carrying assault rifles filled up the truck and peeled out of there. Once they were gone he scanned the ocean of faces for Ava.

"Ava!"

Chapter 18

The C4 obliterated them. Minutes earlier, Marlin had driven at the onslaught of Jeeps and trucks heading his way before diving out of the truck at the last minute and letting it plow into them. Even those that attempted to swerve were blindsided by the blast. Pressing that detonator switch gave him more than a great deal of satisfaction. It was justice. For Amanda, and for every life they had taken since daring to step foot on American soil.

Dirt and chunks of hot metal rained down, tearing through the flesh of the enemy. Running at a hunch, the five of them fanned out in combat intervals. Any who weren't killed in the blast were immediately taken care of as they opened fire on them.

Rounds zipped away from approaching Russian and Korean foot soldiers, kicking up the earth, and peppering concrete walls. He leapt over a short wall and took cover from an armada of bullets whizzing overhead. Marlin took off a grenade from his jacket, kissed it, ripped the pin and cut the corner to take in the sight of those bastards.

"Heads up!" he yelled before tossing it. The moment it exploded he scrambled to his feet, then darted out while unloading as many rounds as he could squeeze off.

They had made it as far as Bishop Plaza. Though they had cut down multiple soldiers it didn't seem to matter. Like rats coming out of sewers, they just kept coming. It was in that moment he realized the full gravity of the situation they were in.

Marlin was pinned down behind a sign that read: Sierra Reality Services. It was part of a red building at the entrance of the plaza. It appeared to be a one-story red brick home that had been turned into a place of business. There were two sliding glass doors behind him. He turned and fired his weapon at the glass, shattering it. He wiggled his way across the ground before scrambling in for cover.

With all the bullets flying overhead he was liable to get hit if he remained out in the open. No sooner had he entered than a grenade landed and rolled across the floor. Marlin lunged over the top of a sofa as it erupted sending shards of hot metal in every direction. That was followed by a smoke grenade and then two soldiers burst in and opened fire. One of them had a flamethrower. He raked it back and forth as it shot out tongues of fire catching every inch of the walls and furniture alight. Assuming that he was dead, they backed out leaving the place ablaze. Marlin coughed hard, and pulled his top up over the bottom of his face. The air was heavy with black, toxic smoke. If he didn't get out of there fast he'd burn up with it all. Using both hands he pulled himself along the floor, then scrambled to his feet and bolted out a door that led him into back offices. His eyes stung, and he groped around as he tried to find his way out. It was getting hotter inside and he could barely catch his breath. When his hands felt glass ahead of him, he reared back and fired three rounds into it, and then stumbled out into the night.

No sooner had he made it out of the back than a round hit him in the shoulder, spinning him to the ground. He didn't even have time to process the pain. A man's voice crying out was what he heard first before a soldier came into view lunging at him with a machete. On his back, he raised his hand and squeezed out two rounds from a Glock. They punched through the man's face and the soldier collapsed on him, covering him in warm, sticky blood.

As he turned his head and tried pushing the guy off, he spotted Todd farther away, running for the cover of some vehicle across the lot. Like witnessing a train wreck in slow motion, he saw rounds cut into his back buckling his legs.

"No!" Marlin screamed.

* * *

"What's our ETA?"

"Ten minutes, Sarge," Brooks yelled back.

"Can't this thing go any faster?"

"I'm giving it everything it's got," Parker said. The

engine roared, the smell of oil and gas filling his nostrils. Westbury was at his wits' end. Exhausted from battling a hardened, skillful group of Russians, they were now barreling south on Highway 395 heading for Bishop. They had lost another three men and were stripped down to fourteen. He hated to leave their bodies behind but this was a different war, and at least they were on U.S. soil. Besides, the odds of any of them surviving were low. Brooks had been trying to reach Griffin and Vaughn since they'd informed them of their plans. He'd tried to persuade that hard-headed cop over the radio but he wouldn't listen. As much as he felt responsible for the loss of American life, he couldn't force people to obey his orders. Law and order was gone from the country and all that remained was a military force that was making its own decisions. How many platoons had been cut down? How many were still surviving across the United States? One thing was for sure, if any Marines were still alive they would keep fighting until their last breath.

* * *

You can do this. You must do this. Move or he will die. After a fierce assault, a rocket launcher had taken out the rear of the truck sending the entire steel frame into a death roll. They were heading north on Barlow Lane to regroup with Marlin's team when they were blindsided crossing Diaz Lane. The truck was wrapped around a power line and tongues of red and orange had enveloped the engine. Chase was upside down when he came to and he could hear bellowing and gunfire but was unable to make sense of the jumbled noise and fragmented images.

He blinked hard, coughed and turned to his side. Matt was unconscious, a large gash on his head. Ahead of him the windshield was cracked and the outside barely visible. In the midst of the chaos he could hear Rodriguez's voice sounding like a radio station slightly out of synch. His mind dialed in until he heard her words clearly.

"Give me your hand. Chase! Chase!"

Headlights washed over the vehicle.

"There's too many," Donahue shouted.

Instead of giving her his hand, he took a hold of Matt and used all his strength to haul him over the top of him.

"Take him. Get him out."

She didn't argue and within seconds she had pulled his limp body out and dragged him a safe distance from the flames. Chase could feel the heat as fire began melting through the dashboard and dropping hot liquidized plastic to the floor. The air inside was becoming unbreathable. Outside Dolman and Donahue were putting up one hell of a fight, tossing every grenade they had in an attempt to wipe out multiple soldiers. The only thing protecting them from bullets slamming into the sides of the truck was the twisted steel. Rodriguez raced back to Chase to help him out but his pant leg was caught on one of the pedals. She leaned in and retrieved a knife and began cutting into the cloth until he felt himself drop a little.

"Now let's get you out."

As she said that a round speared the passenger

window and punched into her arm. She screamed in agony and recoiled. Chase slid out the driver's side onto concrete covered in shards of glass. Pieces stuck into the palms of his hands causing them to bleed.

"We gotta go," Donahue yelled. "This truck might ignite."

Easier said than done. Matt was still unconscious and Rodriguez was now bleeding heavily. As soon as he was on his feet, he shook away the dizziness and swung his rifle around to assist them. While Rodriguez used her good arm and Dolman covered them, Donahue and Chase went over to Matt and hauled him up. Chase tried to get him to wake up but he was out cold. With an arm over each of their shoulders, they had to drag him while shooting at the same time. Several times they tripped and stumbled back. There was a white one-story house just a few yards down from them. Dolman tossed out a few smoke grenades and one more regular grenade to push them back before they made a break for it.

* * *

Gunfire continued all around him and rounds splintered through residents bringing many of them down. As much as they needed to seek out cover, he had to find her. Frantically, Brody elbowed his way through the mass searching for her face. Kai shouted out her name as they went. Brody darted in and out, wishing he still had that photo to show people. It was like being in a football stadium with people rushing to and fro. Some were fleeing to escape the guards who continued to rain down rounds, while others engaged with the enemy, even to the point of losing their lives.

A Russian soldier fell from a height and landed two feet away, a puddle of blood forming around his head.

"Brody!" Kai shouted pointing farther down to where a large group of kids were screaming. He changed the magazine in the rifle, and chambered a round as he ran over to check. With every few steps forward he squeezed off a round or two. As soldiers dropped or turned to flee, Americans cut them down and trampled them beneath their boots. Bodies were everywhere, foreign and American. Was Ava among them? The very thought made him sick to his stomach. It was only made worse by the sight of the injured groping around on the ground, moaning in agony.

He was twenty yards from a section that had been enclosed for young kids when he caught sight of a familiar face in the ocean of eyes. *Cyrus.* Brody gritted his teeth, hatred getting the better of him. He turned his attention towards him and pushed his way through the crowd. He heard the faint sound of Kai calling his name but it was quickly blocked out by his rage.

When he was twenty feet away, Cyrus noticed him. His eyes widened in horror and he turned to flee.

"Cyrus!" Brody yelled but his voice was smothered by the constant barrage of gunfire. He raised his rifle to shoot at him but there were just too many innocents in between. "Shit!" Picking up the pace he plowed into people knocking many to the ground in his pursuit.

An opening emerged in the crowd and he hurried forward. Cyrus who wasn't armed was pushing people over to try and slow Brody down. As he breached the perimeter of the grounds and crossed into the parking lot, he disappeared around a corner. Out of breath, Brody finally got through the crowd and was scanning the immediate area. The threat of soldiers was still at the forefront of his mind, but so was Cyrus getting hold of a weapon. He hugged the wall of a storage unit moving down to the far corner. As he reached the end he snuck a peek around the side, and then heard movement from above. As Brody jerked his head back, Cyrus came crashing down, knocking him to the ground and sending the rifle sliding across the asphalt. He slammed his fist into the side of Brody's ribs keeping a knee on his back.

"You want to kill me?"

Again he drove his fist into the side of his ribs, this time even harder. Brody groaned in agony. Stopping for a second, he must have glanced up as he made a move for the rifle and ran towards it. Worst mistake he could have made. Brody rolled over onto his back, pulled the Beretta from his waistband and shot him from behind. Cyrus slammed against the ground, letting out a guttural, inhuman cry. As Brody rose to his feet, Cyrus was clawing his way over to the rifle that was but a foot from his grasp. Gripping his side, he staggered over to him with his handgun pointed at him. Cyrus was groaning and wheezing. Brody pressed his foot down on Cyrus's hand just as he grasped the butt of the rifle. He twisted his boot, cutting the skin on his hand. Again, he let out a screech.

"I wasn't meant to—"

Before he could finish, Brody took out his knife and drove it down through the back of his neck and out the other side. He said nothing to Cyrus, but let his actions speak for him. He yanked free the blade, took his handgun and fired a shot into the back of his skull.

"Shut the fuck up."

Everyone had final last words, and he was sick of hearing excuses.

* * *

Kai waded through the bodies, scanning faces for

what felt like ages until he spotted her. She was laying on the ground in a fetal position with her hands over her ears. Kai rushed over to her and bent down. She screamed when he took a hold of her hands.

"It's okay, Ava, it's me."

All around them the war intensified, though now the troops had more to contend with. Every able-bodied American was fighting back, whether that was with a gun, a piece of steel bar or bare hands. The resilience in the face of certain death was more than admirable, it was amazing. It brought a smile to Kai's face as he scooped up Ava and carried her through the crowd.

"Where's my dad?"

"He's here."

Really, he had no idea where he'd gone or whether he was still alive. The last time he saw him he was chasing after Cyrus. They moved through the crowd of violence, heading in the same direction he'd seen him in.

No sooner had they made it to the end of the field than Brody came around the corner, his rifle hanging down from his hand, a bloodied knife clutched in the other. He looked a mess but it didn't matter to Ava. Kai put her down and she sprinted the short distance to him. Brody wrapped his arms around her and hugged her tight. His eyes squeezed tightly before opening them and looking at Kai over Ava's shoulder.

He mouthed the words *thank you* before burying his face in her neck.

Chapter 19

His shoulder was in excruciating pain. After sliding out from under the dead soldier, his fatigues were drenched in blood. He cast a sideways glance to check on Todd but he wasn't moving. All around the sound of gunfire intensified, and yet now it seemed as if the troops were coming under fire from behind. Staying low, he pressed down behind a short wall and sat with his eyes partly open watching soldiers rush back and forth. If anyone saw him they would assume he was dead with the amount of blood on him. He just needed a moment to catch his breath. How long he sat there was unknown. Time seemed to cease. There was nothing more than a repetitive cycle of rounds erupting.

Get up, get up, Todd! He nearly blurted it out.

Marlin grabbed his rifle and checked the magazine before moving out. As soon as he came out from the wall, it was game on. He cut down three Russians who were gunning for Daniel, Vaughn and Griffin who had taken up a position inside the Rite-Aid pharmacy. All the windows were shattered, and all that could be seen in the darkness was muzzle flashes.

"Daniel, cover me," he shouted as he rushed towards Todd. Daniel burst out of the store along with the two Marines and fanned out to provide cover. As Marlin crossed the lot towards Todd, he could see the Koreans and Russians engaging with more Americans from behind them. *Yes!* They were not alone in the fight. That gave him a sudden boost of confidence as he dropped down beside Todd.

"Todd."

He was still alive but barely. He'd been shot up really bad. Multiple gunshot wounds to his legs, sides and arms. Blood was trickling out the corner of his mouth as he turned him over. His eyes were glassy. "Come on buddy, stay with me."

Todd looked as if he wanted to say something but he was having a hard enough time breathing. Marlin slipped his arms underneath his pits and began to drag him. A task that wasn't easy. Todd was heavy and it was cumbersome trying to shift even a few feet. Several times he collapsed beneath him. It didn't help that he was having to fire his weapon every few seconds at approaching soldiers.

After he collapsed for the third time, Vaughn came racing over and gave him a hand lugging Todd back to the safety of the pharmacy. They laid him down in the darkness and Marlin was about to try and deal with his wounds when he noticed Todd wasn't breathing.

"No, no, no. Todd."

He pulled off his vest, tore his shirt open but it was a mess. Vaughn moved in behind him and placed a hand on his shoulder. "Nothing you can do. He's gone. We need to move."

Marlin stared at Todd's face. A flash of memories from his childhood. His voice. The jokes. The arguments. The bond. Marlin ran his hand over his eyelids to close them. No words could convey the loss. He was the closest thing to a brother.

"Come on," Vaughn said pulling at Marlin. "I know it's hard but we got to keep moving." An explosion behind them snapped him back into the present moment. Dust and smoke billowed in through the open window frames. As he rose to his feet still looking at Todd, anger swirled inside, the pain in his shoulder had faded into the background. He didn't want to leave him there but they had no other choice. Time was against them and it was heating up outside.

Without hesitation, Marlin pushed his night vision goggles back into place and centered the scope of his rifle on the enemy darting in and out of the parking lot. Each time he squeezed off a round and brought one down, he muttered under his breath, "That's for Todd."

After another fifteen minutes of intense fighting, something shifted. The enemy soldiers no longer were focusing their attention on them, or even a group of Americans that unloaded from a truck farther down. That's when they saw them. Marlin teared up as they came into view.

"Hell yeah!" Daniel shouted. "Here they are. Go get 'em, guys!"

Two military armored trucks came into view, either side Marines were opening fire on the enemy. Grenades flew through the air and sent Koreans spinning like bowling pins. Someone fired a rocket launcher and it struck a Jeep that had a huge machine gun on the back. It exploded and crippled one of the enemy's most devastating weapons. The damn thing had been punching holes in everything in sight.

Marlin and the others raced up to meet them. Behind the cover of one of the vehicles, they met with the sergeant.

"Sergeant Westbury. Griffin Petersen." He shook his hand. "Glad to see you made it."

"It was one hell of a journey." They were yelling loudly over the noise of the guns. "I can't believe you guys managed to hold them off this long."

"We had a little help," Vaughn said turning to

Marlin and Daniel.

"Are they the only ones alive?"

That's when Marlin chimed in. "We have other friends east and south of here. We need to get to them."

A hail of gunfire had all of them ducking.

Vaughn turned to Westbury. "Look, once we push back this group of assholes, give me five men and we'll head southeast. We'll push them back and hopefully the residents who appear to be attacking from the east will either cripple them or force them to surrender."

"I admire your positivity, soldier, but these animals don't surrender."

"Then it's their funeral."

More explosions erupted around them and like that they were back in the fight.

* * *

The walls of the clapboard home were peppered with rounds. Specks of light from the moon filtered in, creating strange abstract patterns on the hardwood floorboards. Chase was beginning to wonder if any of them were going to get out of this alive. Matt was still out cold even though he'd tried to wake him. Beyond the shattered window, he could see the silhouettes of soldiers darting back and forth behind their vehicles.

"How much ammo you got?" Dolman shouted over to Chase.

"I'm nearly out. One more magazine. You?"

"I'm out."

"Here, use this." Rodriguez slid across the floor Matt's Glock 21.

Suddenly Donahue screamed as glass shattered and embedded in the side of his face. He reacted by sticking his M16 out the window and unloading a crazy number of rounds.

"Donahue, save your bullets."

"Fuck that."

Everyone was feeling the pressure. Nowhere felt safe. Chase kept taking a quick look every ten seconds to see what they were up to out there. His greatest fear was they would fire a rocket launcher.

"We need to get out of here," Dolman said.

"Really? No shit, Einstein."

At the rear of the house, they heard glass breaking.

"They're coming in the back." Chase scrambled, staying low and running at a crouch into the hallway and heading for the kitchen where he could hear the commotion. Snagging a grenade off his jacket, he didn't even look to see who it was. Once the pin was out, he tossed it, heard it roll and then drywall filled the air like flour. In those few seconds he slid across the floor and spotted the boots of several more soldiers heading in the back entrance. He fired a burst at their legs. A few screams resounded and they dropped. He was quick to finish them.

Chase prowled through the darkness, hugging the sides of the wall, expecting more of them to enter at any moment. His heart was hammering in his chest. The sound of glass crunching beneath boots got his attention. It was coming from the next room. Quietly he ventured back out into the hallway and slid his gun into his holster.

He wanted to conserve ammo. Switching out for a serrated blade, he stopped and listened. He could hear heavy breathing and then two Russian voices.

More gunfire came from the front of the house. He pressed his back against the wall as he waited for them to emerge. He saw the foot first and the barrel of a gun. In one smooth motion he swung around with that knife and drove it into the man's throat, while shoving the barrel to one side. It erupted in a staccato rhythm peppering the wall. Chase roared as he pushed back with all his might, forcing the soldier into the one behind. They stumbled and landed hard on a glass table, shattering it. Before the second man had a chance to fire off a shot, he retracted the blade and drove it deep into his chest, twisting it and watching the eyes of the enemy widen. He yanked the blade and drove it in again before even a gasp escaped his lips. Then he did it again, and again and again until he was covered in blood and his rage had subsided.

A sudden noise came from behind him and Chase reacted by grabbing his pistol and flipping over. A split second, and he would have fired a round into Dolman.

His hands were shaking and adrenaline was pumping through every fiber of his being.

"Chase, Matt's awake," Rodriguez shouted from the front of the house.

Back up on his feet he staggered back. Matt was sitting up when he came into the room.

"I'm out of ammo," Donahue said. "Shit."

Rodriguez was holding a few fingers up in front of Matt and asking him how many he could see. When he answered correctly she went back to watching the windows and squeezing off a few rounds.

"Son. You okay?"

Matt leaned in and hugged Chase. It had been a long time since he'd hugged his son. Though he was older now, neither one of them had been in a situation like this. The sense of impeding death was at the forefront of everyone's mind.

"Where are we?"

He brought him up to speed on what happened.

"Are we gonna get out of here?"

Chase didn't want to cherry coat it, yet at the same time they weren't dead so they weren't going to give up. Rodriguez was down to her last magazine, as was Chase. There were still a good number of soldiers who'd taken up position behind armored vehicles outside. It would only be a matter of time before they realized they were out, and then they would charge the house.

"I love yah, son," Chase said gripping his son's head against his chest and taking a moment to say the words that meant the most.

"Hey. Hey!" Donahue started getting all hyper as if Christmas had come early. "Look!" Chase scrambled to the window and looked out to see that the troops they were fighting had turned and were now returning fire on another group that was coming from the east. It was hard to tell who it was, or how many there were but anything that distracted them from attacking was a good sign.

In the excitement of watching them come under attack from another opposing force, no one had heard the

Korean enter the rear of the home. Then came the sound of metal rattling across the hardwood floor, and Dolman's voice.

"Grenade!"

The world seemed to slow in that moment. Chase whirled around with his rifle squeezing off a burst. The bullets tore through the attacking soldier just as Dolman dived in the air and landed on top of the grenade. A loud pop, and Dolman's body lifted, then dropped. A puddle of blood slowly seeped out from beneath Dolman. When the dust settled, they looked on in horror at the realization of the sacrifice he'd just made for them all.

Chapter 20

Warfare raged for the better part of the night before silence returned to the once peaceful city of Bishop. Many lives were lost in those chaotic, early morning hours. As dawn broke, and a warm sun rose over the jagged mountains surrounding Mono County, the full extent of the battle between U.S. and foreign troops sank in.

The streets were littered with the corpses of men, women and even children. It would take days before the dead would receive a proper burial and those who were fortunate to survive would have a chance to fully grieve. The death toll would later be numbered in the high hundreds. The attack by troops from North Korea and Russia on the two small communities was only the beginning of a larger battle that still went on in cities and small towns throughout the nation. Though hard to comprehend, and difficult to live through, not all of it was a loss. The sudden wave of attacks had shaken residents to the core and dragged them out of complacency. No longer would they stand by bickering with one another over what one had, and another didn't. A sense of unity could be felt, and courage sparked by the selfless acts of a handful of Mammoth residents. None of them felt like heroes, neither did they go in expecting to be honored for what they had done. Their reward came from watching those who would have never taken up arms, now standing by ready to wage war at a moment's notice.

A shift had occurred, and one that was badly needed if the country was to win.

Days later, still battered, bruised and sporting bandaged wounds, Brody and the others stood around the fresh graves of Todd and Dolman. Dolman's wife and Nancy wept hard, comforted by Rodriguez whose arm was up in a sling. Brody stood clutching Ava's hand after being asked to say a few words about Todd and Dolman.

A cold wind nipped at his skin, and though he was physically present and hearing every word of what each person had shared, he couldn't help but think of the past and the two friends they'd lost that day.

With a heavy heart, and a mind distracted by worries of the future, he tried to push what he couldn't control to one side. He squeezed his eyes shut forcing down the emotion otherwise he wouldn't have been able to speak. He gazed at the fresh mounds of soil and the two crosses that had been inserted at the head of each one.

"One of these men I knew my entire life, the other, only for a matter of months." He paused and swallowed hard. "How do you measure the depth of friendship? Is it measured by the time spent with another? The challenges shared? The hurdles faced? Is it determined by what we know or don't about each other? Is it found in the depth of interactions, the loyalty and willingness to sacrifice? Or is it something more? Something that goes beyond time, words or actions?" Brody felt Ava squeeze his hand. She glanced up at him, her lip curled ever so slightly. A strained but reassuring smile. "Who knows? But one thing I'm certain of, is that these were two of the best men I've ever had the privilege to meet." Brody's brow furrowed. "God speed."

As the group walked away, the wind howled while fallen leaves blew across the ground like tumbleweed marking the end of a season, and the beginning of the next. Change was in the air.

"Brody, a word?" Sergeant Westbury asked. He was off to one side with several Marines. He kept hold of his daughter's hand and told Chase he wouldn't be long.

"You know, what you and your friends did back there was... um..."

"Reckless?"

He smiled. "I was going to say brave but now that I think about it, I have yet to see anyone do anything brave that didn't involve some degree of recklessness." He breathed in the crisp air. He blew out his cheeks and gazed around at the hardened landscape. "One hell of a year this has been, right?"

Brody nodded slowly. "I'm sorry for those you

lost."

"Likewise."

"Where will you head next?" Brody asked.

"We've been in contact with another platoon in Ridgecrest. The war goes on but with the help of people like yourself, I think we stand a chance. You should consider coming. We could use a few more good men."

He didn't know whether he was joking or not.

Brody squinted and swallowed hard. "We're not exactly soldier material."

"I beg to differ. Being a soldier isn't about wearing the uniform, or holding a gun. It's about being ready to lay down your life for another. Standing in the gap when others won't. Running towards the enemy when fear would try to hold you back."

Brody shrugged and glanced down at Ava then back towards the huge group of armed residents that had gathered to bury their own dead. "Thanks, Sergeant, but I think this is where we belong. Like you said, the war goes on but with the help of others, we stand a chance."

"So you'll keep fighting?"

"For as long as it takes."

And that was the truth. He shook his hand and turned towards the mass of faces full of grit and purpose. Weeks prior they would have killed each other to survive and now here they were, working together towards one cause — freedom.

* * *

THANK YOU FOR READING

War Buds 3: Overcome

A Plea

Thank you for reading War Buds 3: Overcome. If you enjoyed the book, I would really appreciate it if you would consider leaving a review. Without reviews, an author's books are virtually invisible on the retail sites. It also lets me know what you liked. You can leave a review by visiting the book's page. I would greatly appreciate it. It only takes a couple of seconds.

Thank you — **Jack Hunt**

Newsletter

Thank you for buying War Buds 3: Overcome published by Direct Response Publishing.

Click here to receive special offers, bonus content, and news about new Jack Hunt's books. Sign up for the newsletter. http://www.jackhuntbooks.com/signup/

About the Author

Jack Hunt is the author of horror, sci-fi and post-apocalyptic novels. He currently has three books out in the Camp Zero series, five books out in the Renegades series, three books in the Agora Virus series, one out in the Armada series, a time travel book called Killing Time and another called Mavericks: Hunters Moon. Jack lives on the East coast of North America.

Made in the USA
Monee, IL
12 December 2019